PENGUI

Maigr

'Extr

'A brilliant writer'

        – India Knight

'Intense atmosphere and resonant detail . . . make Simenon's fiction remarkably like life'

        – Julian Barnes

'A truly wonderful writer . . . marvellously readable – lucid, simple, absolutely in tune with the world he creates'

        – Muriel Spark

'Few writers have ever conveyed with such a sure touch, the bleakness of human life'

        – A. N. Wilson

'Compelling, remorseless, brilliant'

        – John Gray

'A writer of genius, one whose simplicity of language creates indelible images that the florid stylists of our own day can only dream of'

        – *Daily Mail*

'The mysteries of the human personality are revealed in all their disconcerting complexity'

        – Anita Brookner

'One of the greatest writers of our time'

        – *The Sunday Times*

'I love reading Simenon. He makes me think of Chekhov'

        – William Faulkner

'One of the great psychological novelists of this century'

        – *Independent*

'The greatest of all, the most genuine novelist we have had in literature'

        – André Gide

'Simenon ought to be spoken of in the same breath as Camus, Beckett and Kafka'

        – *Independent on Sunday*

ABOUT THE AUTHOR

Georges Simenon was born on 12 February 1903 in Liège, Belgium, and died in 1989 in Lausanne, Switzerland, where he had lived for the latter part of his life. Between 1931 and 1972 he published seventy-five novels and twenty-eight short stories featuring Inspector Maigret.

Simenon always resisted identifying himself with his famous literary character, but acknowledged that they shared an important characteristic:

> My motto, to the extent that I have one, has been noted often enough, and I've always conformed to it. It's the one I've given to old Maigret, who resembles me in certain points . . . 'understand and judge not'.

Penguin is publishing the entire series of Maigret novels.

GEORGES SIMENON

Maigret's Mistake

Translated by HOWARD CURTIS

PENGUIN BOOKS

PENGUIN CLASSICS

UK | USA | Canada | Ireland | Australia
India | New Zealand | South Africa

Penguin Books is part of the Penguin Random House group of companies
whose addresses can be found at global.penguinrandomhouse.com

First published in French as *Maigret se trompe* by Presses de la Cité 1953
This translation first published 2017
001

Set in Dante MT Std 12.5/15pt
Typeset in India by Thomson Digital Pvt Ltd, Noida, Delhi
Printed in Great Britain by Clays Ltd, St Ives plc

ISBN: 978-0-241-27984-7

www.greenpenguin.co.uk

Maigret's Mistake

1.

It was 8.25 in the morning, and Maigret was just getting up from the table, still finishing his last cup of coffee. Even though it was only November, the lights were on. At the window, Madame Maigret had to strain to see passers-by hurrying to work through the fog, their hands in their pockets, their backs stooped.

'I think you should put your thick overcoat on,' she said.

Because it was by observing people in the street that she knew what the weather was like outside. They were all walking quickly that morning, many wearing scarves, and they had a characteristic way of stamping their feet on the pavement to warm themselves. She had seen several wiping their noses.

'I'll get it for you.'

He still had his cup in his hand when the telephone rang. Picking up the receiver, he, too, now looked outside. The houses opposite were almost invisible through the yellowish cloud that had descended over the streets during the night.

'Hello? Detective Chief Inspector Maigret? . . . Dupeu here, from the Ternes district . . .'

It was curious that it should be Dupeu calling him, because he was probably the man most in tune with the atmosphere of that morning. Dupeu was the chief inspector at the Rue de l'Étoile police station. He squinted. His wife squinted. It was said that his three daughters, whom Maigret didn't know, also squinted. He was a conscientious official, so anxious to do the right thing that he almost made himself sick. He made even the objects around him seem dull, and even though you knew he was the best man in the world, you couldn't help avoiding him. Not to mention that he always had a cold, winter and summer.

'I'm sorry to bother you at home. I assumed you hadn't left yet, so I said to myself . . .'

You just had to wait. He needed to explain himself. He invariably felt the need to explain why he was doing this or that, as if he felt he was at fault.

'. . . I know you always like to be there personally. I may be wrong, but I have the impression this is quite an unusual case. Mind you, I don't know much myself yet. I've only just arrived.'

Madame Maigret was waiting, the overcoat in her hand, and her husband said under his breath, to stop her getting too impatient, 'Dupeu!'

Dupeu was still speaking in a monotonous voice. 'I got to my office at eight o'clock as usual and was just going through the early mail when, at eight minutes past, I received a telephone call from the cleaning lady. She was the one who found the body when she entered the apartment on Avenue Carnot. As it's so close, I came straight here with my secretary.'

'A murder?'

'It could just possibly be suicide, but I'm convinced it's murder.'

4

'Who is it?'

'A young woman named Louise Filon. I've never heard of her.'

'I'm on my way.'

Dupeu began talking again, but Maigret, pretending not to notice, had already hung up. Before leaving, he called Quai des Orfèvres and asked to be put through to Criminal Records.

'Is Moers there? . . . Yes, call him to the phone . . . Hello, is that you, Moers? Could you go straight to Avenue Carnot with your men? . . . A murder . . . I'll see you there . . .'

He gave them the number of the building, put on his overcoat, and, a few moments later, there was one more dark figure walking quickly through the fog. It wasn't until he got to the corner of Boulevard Voltaire that he found a taxi.

The avenues around Place de l'Étoile were almost deserted. Men were collecting the dustbins. Most of the curtains were still closed, and there were lights in only a few of the windows.

On Avenue Carnot, an officer in a cape was standing on the pavement, but no crowd of onlookers had formed.

'Which floor?' Maigret asked him.

'Third.'

He walked through the main door with its highly polished brass handles. The lights were on in the lodge, where the concierge was having her breakfast. She looked at him through the window but didn't get up. The lift worked noiselessly, as in any well-maintained building. The carpets on the polished oak stairs were a fine deep red.

On the third floor, he was confronted with three doors and was hesitating when the one on the left opened. Dupeu was there, his nose red, just as Maigret had expected to see him.

'Come in. I thought it best not to touch anything until you arrived. I haven't even questioned the cleaning lady.'

Crossing the entrance hall, where there was only a coat stand and two chairs, they entered a living room, where the lights were on.

'The cleaning lady was immediately surprised when she saw the light.'

In the corner of a yellow sofa, a brown-haired young woman lay slumped in a curious position, with a large dark-red stain on her dressing gown.

'She was shot in the head. The shot seems to have been fired from behind and very close. As you see, she didn't fall.'

She had simply collapsed on to her right-hand side, and her head was dangling, her hair almost touching the carpet.

'Where's the cleaning lady?'

'In the kitchen. She asked me if she could make herself a cup of coffee. She says she got here at eight o'clock, as she does every morning. She has a key to the apartment. She came in, saw the body, claims she didn't touch anything and immediately phoned.'

It was only now that Maigret realized what he had found strange when he arrived. Normally, he would have had to get through a line of onlookers out on the pavement. Usually, too, the tenants are gathered on the landings, looking on. Here, though, everything was as calm as if nothing had happened.

'Is the kitchen through there?'

He found it at the end of a corridor. The door was open. A darkly dressed woman with black hair and eyes was sitting by the gas stove, drinking a cup of coffee, blowing on the liquid to cool it.

Maigret had the feeling he had met her before. Frowning, he looked at her closely, while she calmly sustained his gaze and continued drinking. She was very short. Sitting, her feet barely touched the floor, and she was wearing shoes that were too big for her, while her dress was too loose and too long.

'I think we know each other,' he said.

'That's quite possible,' she replied without flinching.

'What's your name?'

'Désirée Brault.'

The name Désirée put him on the right track.

'Were you ever arrested for shoplifting in department stores?'

'Among other things.'

'What else?'

'I've been arrested so many times!'

Her face expressed no fear. In fact, it expressed nothing. She looked at him, answered his questions, but as for what she was thinking, that was impossible to guess.

'Have you done time?'

'You'll find all that in my record.'

'Prostitution?'

'What of it?'

A long time ago, evidently. Now, she must be about fifty or sixty. She was emaciated. Her hair wasn't white, or even greying, but it had become sparse, and you could see the skull through it.

'There was a time when I was as good as any other woman!'

'How long have you been working in this apartment?'

'Next month will make a year. I started in December, not long before Christmas.'

'Are you here all day?'

'Just from eight to twelve.'

The coffee smelled so good that Maigret poured himself a cup. Inspector Dupeu was standing timidly in the doorway.

'Would you like some, Dupeu?'

'No, thanks. I had breakfast less than an hour ago.'

Désirée Brault stood up to pour herself another cup, too. Her dress hung loosely from her body. She probably weighed no more than a fourteen-year-old.

'Do you work in other places?'

'Three or four. It varies from week to week.'

'Do you live alone?'

'With my husband.'

'Has he been in prison, too?'

'Never. He just drinks.'

'Doesn't he work?'

'He hasn't worked a single day in fifteen years, not even to hammer a nail into a wall.'

She said this without bitterness, in a steady voice in which it was hard to detect any irony.

8

'What happened this morning?'

She made a movement of her head to indicate Dupeu.

'Didn't he tell you? All right, then. I got here at eight o'clock.'

'Where do you live?'

'Near Place Clichy. I took the Métro. I opened the door with my key and noticed there was a light on in the living room.'

'Was the living-room door open?'

'No.'

'Was your employer usually still in bed when you arrived in the morning?'

'She didn't get up till around ten, sometimes later.'

'What did she do?'

'Nothing.'

'Carry on.'

'I opened the living-room door and saw her.'

'Did you touch her?'

'I didn't need to touch her to know she was dead. Have you ever seen anyone walking around with half their face shot off?'

'What did you do then?'

'I called the police station.'

'You didn't alert the neighbours, or the concierge?'

She shrugged.

'Why should I have done that?'

'What did you do after you phoned?'

'I waited.'

'Doing what?'

'Doing nothing.'

It was staggering in its simplicity. She had simply stayed there, waiting for the doorbell to ring, perhaps looking at the body.

'Are you sure you didn't touch anything?'

'Quite sure.'

'Did you find a gun?'

'I didn't find anything.'

Dupeu intervened.

'We looked everywhere for the weapon, but there was no sign of it.'

'Did Louise Filon own a gun?'

'If she did, I never saw it.'

'Are there any pieces of furniture that are kept locked?'

'No.'

'I assume you know what's in the cupboards?'

'Yes.'

'And you never saw a gun?'

'No, never.'

'Tell me, did your employer know you'd been in prison?'

'I told her everything.'

'Didn't that bother her?'

'It amused her. I don't know if she also did time, but she might have done.'

'What do you mean?'

'That before she came to live here, she was on the game.'

'How do you know that?'

'Because she told me. Even if she hadn't told me . . .'

There was the sound of shuffling on the landing, and Dupeu went and opened the door. It was Moers and his men, with their equipment.

'Don't start straight away,' Maigret said to Moers. 'Phone the prosecutor while you're waiting for me to finish up here.'

Désirée Brault fascinated him, and so did everything that could be sensed behind her words. He took off his coat, because he felt hot, and sat down, continuing to drink his coffee in little sips.

'Wouldn't you like to sit down?'

'I'd love to. It isn't often a cleaning lady gets asked to sit.'

And this time, she almost smiled.

'Do you have any idea who might have killed your employer?'

'Of course not.'

'Did she have lots of visitors?'

'I never saw any, apart from a local doctor once, when she had bronchitis. Mind you, I leave at twelve.'

'Do you know if she had a boyfriend?'

'All I know is that there are a man's slippers and dressing gown in a wardrobe. A box of cigars, too. She didn't smoke cigars.'

'Do you know who the man is?'

'I never saw him.'

'Do you know his name? Did he ever phone while you were here?'

'Yes, sometimes.'

'What did she call him?'

'Pierrot.'

'Was she a kept woman?'

'I suppose someone had to pay the rent, didn't they? And pay for all the rest.'

Maigret stood up, put his cup down and filled a pipe.

'What do I do now?' she asked.

'Nothing. Just wait.'

He went back to the living room, where the men from Records were awaiting a signal from him to get down to work. The room was tidy. In an ashtray near the sofa, there was cigarette ash, and cigarette ends, too, three in all, including two with lipstick marks on them.

A half-open door led from this room to the bedroom, and Maigret noted with a touch of surprise that the bed was unmade and that there was a hollow in the pillow as if someone had been sleeping there.

'Isn't the doctor here yet?'

'He isn't at home. His wife's phoning around the patients he was due to see this morning.'

He opened a few wardrobes, a few drawers. The clothes and underwear were those of a young woman who dresses without much taste, not the kind you expected to find in an apartment on Avenue Carnot.

'Look for prints and anything else you can find, Moers. I'm going down to talk to the concierge.'

'Do you still need me?' Dupeu asked.

'No. I'm very grateful to you. Send me your report sometime today. You've done a good job, Dupeu.'

'You know, I immediately thought it would interest you. If there'd been a weapon near the sofa, I'd have said it was suicide, because the shot came from such close range. Although women like that usually use Veronal to kill themselves. I haven't known a woman to shoot herself in this neighbourhood for at least five years. So as there isn't any weapon . . .'

'You've done very well, Dupeu.'

'I try the best I can to . . .'

He was still talking as he descended the stairs. Maigret left him on the doormat outside the concierge's door and went into the lodge.

'Good morning, madame.'

'Good morning, inspector.'

'You know who I am?'

She nodded.

'You know what's happened?'

'I asked the officer standing guard out there on the pavement. He told me Mademoiselle Louise is dead.'

The lodge had the comfortable appearance of all concierges' lodges in this area. The concierge herself, who was only in her forties, was well, even smartly dressed. She was actually quite pretty, although her features were slightly too fleshy.

'Was she murdered?' she asked, as Maigret sat down by the window.

'What makes you think that?'

'I don't think the police would be here if she'd died a natural death.'

'She might have killed herself.'

'That wouldn't have been like her.'

'Did you know her well?'

'Not that well. She never lingered in my lodge, just half opened the door as she passed to ask if she had any mail.

13

She didn't really feel at ease in this building, if you know what I mean.'

'You mean she wasn't from the same background as your other tenants?'

'Yes.'

'What do you think her background was?'

'I don't rightly know. I have no reason to speak ill of her. She was quiet, not conceited.'

'Did her cleaning lady ever talk to you about her?'

'Madame Brault and I don't speak to each other.'

'You know her?'

'I have no reason to know her. I see her go up and down. That's enough for me.'

'Was Louise Filon a kept woman?'

'It's possible. She certainly always paid her rent on time.'

'Did she have visitors?'

'Occasionally.'

'But not regularly?'

'Not what I'd call regularly.'

Maigret had the impression there was something holding her back. Unlike Madame Brault, the concierge was nervous and from time to time cast a rapid glance at the glazed door. It was she who announced:

'The doctor's going up.'

'Tell me, madame . . . What's your name, by the way?'

'Cornet.'

'Tell me, Madame Cornet, is there something you're trying to hide from me?'

She made an effort to look him in the eyes.

'Why do you ask that?'

'No reason. I just like to know. Was it always the same man who came to see Louise Filon?'

'It was always the same man I saw pass by here.'

'What kind of man?'

'A musician.'

'How do you know he's a musician?'

'Because once or twice I saw him with a saxophone case under his arm.'

'Did he come last night?'

'Yes, about ten.'

'Did you open the door for him?'

'No. Until I go to bed at eleven, I leave the door open.'

'But you see who comes in?'

'Most of the time. The tenants are quiet. Most of them are important people.'

'You say the musician in question went up at about ten?'

'Yes. He only stayed about ten minutes, and when he left he seemed to be in a hurry. I heard him stride off towards Place de l'Étoile.'

'You didn't see his face, whether he looked upset or . . .'

'No.'

'Did Louise Filon have any other visitors last night?'

'No.'

'So if the doctor discovers that the murder was committed between ten and eleven, for example, it'd be more or less certain that . . .'

'I didn't say that. I said she didn't have any other visitors.'

'Do you think the musician was her lover?'

She didn't reply at once.

'I don't know,' she murmured at last.

'What do you mean?'

'Nothing. I was thinking of the cost of the apartment.'

'You mean he wasn't the kind of musician who could afford to keep his girlfriend in a place like this?'

'That's right.'

'It doesn't seem to surprise you, Madame Cornet, that your tenant has been murdered.'

'I didn't expect it, but it doesn't surprise me either.'

'Why?'

'No particular reason. I have the feeling women like that are more exposed than others. At any rate, that's the impression you get from reading the papers.'

'I'm going to ask you to make me a list of all the tenants who came in or went out after nine o'clock last night. I'll pick it up on my way out.'

'That's easy.'

He left the lodge in time to see the prosecutor and his deputy getting out of a car, together with the court clerk. All three looked cold. The fog had not yet cleared, and the steam from all their breaths mingled with it.

Handshakes. The lift. Apart from the third floor, the building was still as quiet as it had been when Maigret arrived. The people here weren't the kind to watch out for comings and goings behind their half-opened doors, or to gather on the landings because a woman had been killed.

Moers' technicians had set up their equipment all over the apartment, and the doctor had finished examining the body. He shook hands with Maigret.

'What time?' Maigret asked.

'Between nine and midnight, roughly speaking. My guess would be eleven at the latest rather than midnight.'

'I assume death was instantaneous?'

'You saw her. The shot was fired at close range.'

'From behind?'

'From behind, and a little to the side.'

'She seems to have been smoking a cigarette when it happened,' Moers said. 'It fell on the carpet and burned itself out. It's lucky the carpet didn't catch fire.'

'What exactly are we dealing with?' asked the deputy, who knew nothing yet.

'I have no idea. Maybe a straightforward crime, though I'd be surprised.'

'Do you have any ideas?'

'None whatever. I'm going to have another word with the cleaning lady.'

Before reaching the kitchen, he telephoned Quai des Orfèvres and asked Lucas, who was on duty, to join him immediately. After that, he ignored the prosecutors and the technicians, who were continuing with their usual tasks.

Madame Brault had not moved. She was no longer drinking coffee, but was smoking a cigarette, which, given her physique, seemed strange.

'I guess I'm allowed?' she said, following the direction of Maigret's gaze.

He sat down facing her.

'Tell me.'

'Tell you what?'

'Everything you know.'

'I've already told you.'

'How did Louise Filon spend her days?'

'I can only talk about what she did in the morning. She'd get up about ten. Or rather, she'd wake up but wouldn't get up straight away. I'd bring her coffee, and she'd drink it in bed, and smoke and read.'

'What kind of thing did she read?'

'Magazines and novels. She often listened to the radio. You probably noticed one on her bedside table.'

'Did she make any phone calls?'

'At about eleven.'

'Every day?'

'Almost every day.'

'To Pierrot?'

'Yes. Sometimes at midday she'd dress and go out to eat, but that was quite rare. Most of the time, she'd send me to the pork butcher's to buy cold meats or ready-made dishes.'

'Do you have any idea how she spent her afternoons?'

'I assume she went out. She must have gone out because in the morning I'd find dirty shoes. I suppose she did the rounds of the shops, like all women.'

'Did she have dinner at home?'

'There weren't usually any dirty dishes.'

'Do you suppose she went to meet Pierrot?'

'Him or another man.'

'Are you sure you've never seen him?'

'Quite sure.'

'Did you ever see any other men?'

'Only the man from the gas company or a delivery boy.'

'When was the last time you were in prison?'

'Six years ago.'

'Have you lost the taste for shoplifting from department stores?'

'I'm not as fast as I used to be . . . They're taking away the body.'

There were noises from the living room, and it was indeed the men from the Forensic Institute.

'She didn't get to enjoy it for long!'

'What do you mean?'

'I mean she lived in poverty until she was twenty-four and then had barely two good years.'

'Did she confide in you?'

'We chatted like human beings.'

'Did she tell you where she was from?'

'She was born in the eighteenth arrondissement, practically in the street. She spent most of her life around La Chapelle. When she moved here, she thought it was going to be the good life.'

'Wasn't she happy?'

The cleaning lady shrugged, looking at Maigret with a kind of pity, as if surprised that he seemed to show so little understanding. 'Do you think it was fun for her to live in a building like this, where people didn't even condescend to look at her when they passed her on the stairs?'

'Why did she come here?'

'She must have had her reasons.'

'Was it her musician who kept her?'

'Who told you about the musician?'

'It doesn't matter. Is Pierrot a saxophone player?'

'I think so. I know he plays in a dance hall.'

She was only saying what she wanted to say. Now that Maigret had a clearer idea of the kind of girl Louise Filon had been, he felt certain that in the mornings the two women had chatted away to their hearts' content.

'I don't think a dance-hall musician would be in a position to pay the rent of an apartment like this,' he said.

'Neither do I.'

'So?'

'So there must have been someone else,' she said calmly.

'Pierrot came to see her last night.'

She didn't start, continued looking him in the eyes. 'And I assume you've jumped to the conclusion that he was the one who killed her? There's only one thing I can tell you: they loved each other.'

'Did she tell you that?'

'Not only did they love each other, but their one dream was to get married.'

'Why didn't they?'

'Maybe because they didn't have any money. Maybe also because the other man wouldn't let her go.'

'The other man?'

'You know perfectly well I'm talking about the one who paid. Do I have to draw you a picture?'

An idea occurred to Maigret, and he went to the bedroom and opened the wardrobe. From it, he took a pair of men's slippers in frosted kidskin, made to measure by a bootmaker in Rue Saint-Honoré, one of the most expensive in Paris. Taking down the dressing gown, which was of thick maroon silk, he found that it bore the label of a shirt maker in Rue de Rivoli.

Moers' men had already left. Moers himself was waiting for Maigret in the living room.

'What did you find?'

'Prints, obviously, some old, some more recent.'

'Men's prints?'

'One man, at least. We'll have some pictures in an hour.'

'Pass them on to Records. I'd like you to take these slippers and this dressing gown. When you get to headquarters, hand them over to Janvier or Torrence. I'd like them to be shown to the shopkeepers who supplied them.'

'For the slippers, it'll be easy, I assume, because they have an order number on them.'

It was quiet again in the apartment, and Maigret went back to the cleaning lady in the kitchen.

'You don't need to stay here any more.'

'Can I clean?'

'Not yet, not today.'

'What should I do?'

'You can go home. But don't leave Paris. It may be that—'

'All right, got it.'

'Are you sure you have nothing else to tell me?'

'If I remember anything, I'll let you know.'

'One more question: are you sure that, from the time you found the body to the time Inspector Dupeu arrived, you didn't leave the apartment?'

'I swear.'

'And nobody came in?'

'Not a soul.'

She went and took down a shopping bag she probably always carried with her, and Maigret made sure there was no gun in it.

'Search me, if you feel like it.'

He didn't search her, but to set his mind at rest, and not without a touch of embarrassment, he passed his hands over her loose dress.

'That would have given you a thrill in the old days.'

She left, probably passing Lucas on the stairs. His hat and coat were wet.

'Is it raining?'

'It started ten minutes ago. What do you want me to do, chief?'

'I don't know exactly. I'd like you to stay here. If anyone phones, try to find out where the call is coming from. There may be a call at about eleven. Tell the office to put a tap on the line. Apart from that, keep searching here. It's been done, but you never know.'

'What exactly are we dealing with?'

'A girl who used to walk the streets in Barbès and was set up in her own place by someone. As far as we know, she was in love with a dance-hall musician.'

'Was he the one who killed her?'

'He came to see her last night. The concierge says nobody else came up here.'

'Do we have a description of him?'

'I'm going down to question the concierge again.'

The concierge was busy sorting through the second post. According to her, Pierrot was a fair-haired, well-built man of about thirty who looked more like a butcher's boy than a musician.

'Do you have anything else to tell me?'

'No, nothing else, Monsieur Maigret. If I remember anything, I'll let you know.'

It was strange. The same answer, or almost, as the cleaning lady. He was convinced that both women, doubtless for different reasons, were avoiding telling him all they knew.

As he would probably have to walk all the way to Place de l'Étoile to find a taxi, he turned up the collar of his coat and set off, his hands in his pockets like the people Madame Maigret had seen from the window that morning. The fog had turned into a fine, chilly rain of the kind associated with head colds, and he went into a little bar on the corner of the street and ordered a toddy.

2.

It was Janvier who was dealing with Pierrot the musician, reconstructing his movements up until the time he decided to vanish.

Just before 11.30, Lucas, having a quiet poke around the apartment on Avenue Carnot, had at last heard the telephone ring. He had picked up the receiver, taking care not to say anything, and at the other end a man's voice had murmured:

'Is that you?'

Before growing suspicious of the silence that greeted him, Pierrot had added:

'Is there someone with you?'

Finally, in a worried tone:

'Hello? This is Carnot 22-35, isn't it?'

'Carnot 22-35, yes.'

Lucas could hear the man's breathing on the line. He was calling from a public booth, probably in a bar, because there had been the telltale noise of a token falling into the metal box.

At last, after a while, the musician hung up. Then it was only a matter of waiting until the man in the listening room called. It took barely two minutes.

'Lucas? Your man phoned from a bistro called Chez Léon, on the corner of Boulevard Rochechouart and Rue Briquet.'

Immediately, Lucas phoned the Goutte d'Or police station, which was not far from Boulevard Rochechouart.

'May I speak to Inspector Janin?'

As luck would have it, he was in his office. Lucas provided him with a rough description of Pierrot and the name of the bar.

'Do nothing until Janvier joins you.'

He finally got through to Janvier. Meanwhile, it was still raining on this world of stone, brick and concrete through which wove dark figures and umbrellas. Maigret was in his office, his tie loosened, four filled pipes in front of him, finishing a report that had to be handed in by midday. Janvier half opened the door of the office.

'He phoned, chief. We know where he is. Lucas alerted the Goutte d'Or, and Janin should already be there. I'm on my way now. What should I do with him?'

Maigret looked at him with large, tired eyes.

'Bring him to me, and be nice about it.'

'Aren't you going to lunch?'

'I'll have some sandwiches brought up.'

Janvier used one of the little black cars of the Police Judiciaire, getting the driver to stop some distance from the bar. It was a narrow bistro, longer than it was wide, with so much steam on the windows that you couldn't see inside. When he opened the door, he glimpsed Janin waiting for him over a vermouth-cassis. Apart from him, there were only four customers. The tiled floor was covered in sawdust, the walls were a dirty yellow, and the phone booth was next to the toilets.

'Gone?'

Holding out his hand, Janin nodded. The owner, who clearly knew the local officer, asked Janvier in a somewhat ironic voice:

'Would you like a drink?'

'A beer.'

The customers were also looking at them. Janin must have already asked his questions.

'We can talk,' he said in a low voice. 'He came in at a quarter to eleven, as he does every day.'

'Does the owner know his name?'

'All he knows is that he's called Pierrot, that he's a musician and probably lives in the area. He comes here every morning at a quarter to eleven to have his coffee. Almost always, he receives a phone call at eleven o'clock. This morning, he didn't get one. He waited half an hour and then went into the booth. When he came out, he looked worried. He stayed a while longer at the counter, then paid and left.'

'Do we know where he has lunch?'

'The owner claims he doesn't know. Do you still need me?'

'I don't know. Let's go outside.'

Once outside, Janvier glanced along Rue Briquet, which was very short, and where you could see the signs of two hotels that were clearly used by prostitutes.

If Pierrot was in the habit of having his morning coffee in the little bar, there was a good chance he lived nearby.

'Shall we take a look?'

The first hotel was called the Hôtel du Var. To the right of the corridor, there was an office, with an old woman in it.

'Is Pierrot at home?'

As she probably also knew Janin, he took care not to show himself, while of all those at the Police Judiciaire, Janvier was probably the one who looked least like a policeman.

'He went out more than an hour ago.'

'Are you sure he hasn't come back?'

'Positive. I haven't left the office. And besides, his key's on the board.'

She finally saw Janin, who had stepped forwards.

'So that's it! What do you want with the boy?'

'Can I see the register? How long has he been living here?'

'More than a year. He pays monthly.'

She went and fetched the book and leafed through it.

'Here you are. You know this house is above board.'

Pierrot's real name was Pierre Eyraud; he was twenty-nine years old and had been born in Paris.

'What time does he usually get back?'

'Sometimes he comes back early in the afternoon, sometimes not.'

'Does he have women visitors?'

'Like anyone else.'

'Always the same one?'

She did not hesitate for long. She knew that if she didn't toe the line, Janin would have a hundred opportunities to catch her out.

'You must know her, too, Monsieur Janin. She was always hanging around here. It's Lulu.'

'Lulu what?'

'I don't know. I've always called her Lulu. A pretty girl, and a lucky one, too. These days she wears fur coats and all that, and comes here by taxi.'

'Did you see her yesterday?' Janvier asked.

'No, not yesterday, but the day before yesterday. That was Sunday, the day before yesterday, wasn't it? She arrived just after midday with some little packages, and they had lunch in his room. Afterwards, they left arm in arm. I assume they went to the cinema.'

'Give me the key.'

She shrugged. What was the point resisting?

'Try not to make it too obvious you searched his room. He'd blame me for it.'

To be on the safe side – to stop the old woman from phoning Pierre Eyraud and bringing him up to date, for example – Janin stayed downstairs. All the doors were open on the first floor, where the rooms that could be rented for an hour or even less were situated. Further up lived those tenants who rented by the week or the month, and noises could be heard behind the doors; there must be another musician in the hotel, because someone was playing the accordion.

Janvier went into Room 53, which had a view of the courtyard. The bed was of iron, the rug threadbare and discoloured, as was the tablecloth. On the wash-basin was a toothbrush, a tube of toothpaste, a comb, a shaving brush and a razor. In a corner, a big suitcase lay open, used only to put dirty washing in.

Janvier found only one suit in the wardrobe, an old pair of trousers, a grey felt hat and a cap. As for Pierrot's clothes, they consisted merely of three or four shirts, a few pairs of socks and pants. Another drawer was full of sheet music. It was on the bottom shelf of the bedside table that he finally spotted a pair of women's slippers and, hanging behind the door, a salmon-pink crêpe de Chine dressing gown.

By the time he went back downstairs, Janin had had time to chat with the manageress.

'I have the addresses of two or three restaurants where he often has lunch.'

It was only in the street that Janvier took note of them.

'You'd do better to stay here,' he said to Janin. 'When the newspapers come out, he'll find out what happened to his girlfriend, if he doesn't already know. He might drop by the hotel.'

'Do you think it's him?'

'The chief didn't say.'

Janvier headed first for an Italian restaurant on Boulevard Rochechouart, quiet, cosy and smelling of food cooked with herbs. Two waitresses in black and white bustled from table to table, but there was nobody answering to Pierrot's description.

'Have you seen Pierre Eyraud?'

'The musician? No, he hasn't been in. What day is it? Tuesday? I'd be surprised if he came, it isn't his day.'

The second restaurant on the list was a brasserie near the Barbès intersection, and here, too, nobody had seen Pierrot.

There was one last hope, a restaurant frequented by drivers, its front painted yellow and the menu written on a slate hanging on the door. The owner was behind the counter, pouring wine. There was only one waitress, a tall, thin girl, and the owner's wife could be glimpsed in the kitchen.

Janvier approached the tin bar, ordered a beer. Everyone here probably knew each other, because they were watching him curiously.

'I don't have draught beer,' the owner said. 'How about a glass of Beaujolais?'

Janvier nodded, waited a few moments, then asked:

'Has Pierrot been in?'

'The musician?'

'That's right. He arranged to meet me here at a quarter past twelve.'

It was now 12.45.

'If you'd come at a quarter past twelve, you'd have seen him.'

They weren't suspicious. He seemed very natural.

'So he didn't wait for me?'

'To tell the truth, he didn't even finish his lunch.'

'Did someone come to get him?'

'No. He left all of a sudden, saying he was in a hurry.'

'What time was that?'

'About fifteen minutes ago.'

Janvier, looking around the tables, noticed that two of the customers were reading the afternoon paper over their lunch. One table, near the window, hadn't been cleared. And next to a plate still containing veal stew, a newspaper lay open.

'Was he sitting there?'

'Yes.'

Janvier had only 200 metres to walk in the rain to join Janin, who was keeping guard in Rue Briquet.

'Has he been back?'

'I haven't seen anyone.'

'He was in a little restaurant less than half an hour ago. A paper seller came in. Pierrot took one look at the front page and rushed out. I think I'd better call the chief.'

On Maigret's desk at Quai des Orfèvres there was a tray with two huge sandwiches and two glasses of beer. Maigret listened to Janvier's report.

'Try to find out the name of the dance hall where he works. The manageress of the hotel probably knows it. It must be somewhere in the area. I'd like Janin to carry on watching the hotel.'

Maigret was right. The hotel's manageress did know it. She, too, had the newspaper in her office but she hadn't made any connection between the Louise Filon they were talking about and the Lulu she knew. All the newspaper had said in its first edition was:

> Louise Filon, unemployed, was found dead this morning by her cleaning lady in an apartment on Avenue Carnot. She was killed by a gunshot fired at close range, probably sometime last night. Robbery does not appear to have been the motive. Detective Chief Inspector Maigret has taken personal charge of the investigation, and we believe he is already following a lead.

Pierrot worked at the Grelot, a dance hall in Rue Charbonnière, near the corner of Boulevard de La Chapelle.

It was still in the area, although in the less savoury part of it. From Boulevard de La Chapelle onwards Janvier encountered Arabs wandering in the rain looking as if they had nothing to do. There were other men apart from the Arabs, and women, too, waiting for clients in the doorways of hotels in broad daylight, in spite of the regulations.

The front of the Grelot was painted mauve, and by night the light was probably also mauve. At this hour, there was nobody inside except the owner, busy having lunch with a middle-aged woman who might have been his wife. He watched as Janvier, who had closed the door behind him, advanced towards him. Janvier realized that the man had guessed his profession from the first glance.

'What do you want? The bar doesn't open till five.'

Janvier showed his badge, and the owner didn't flinch. He was short and broad, with the nose and ears of a former boxer. Above the dance-floor, there was a kind of balcony, to which the musicians gained access by a ladder.

'I'm listening.'

'Is Pierrot here?'

The other man looked around him at the empty room and merely replied:

'Can you see him?'

'Has he been in today?'

'He starts work at seven in the evening. Sometimes he drops by about four or five to play *belote*.'

'Did he work yesterday?'

Janvier realized that something was up, because the man and the woman looked at each other.

'What has he done?' the owner asked cautiously.

'Maybe nothing. I just want to ask him a few questions.'

'Why?'

Janvier went for broke.

'Because Lulu is dead.'

'What? What are you talking about?'

He was genuinely surprised. True, there was no newspaper in sight.

'Since when?'

'Since last night.'

'What happened to her?'

'Do you know her?'

'She used to be a regular. She was here almost every night. I'm talking about two years ago.'

'And now?'

'She came from time to time, had a drink, listened to the music.'

'What time did Pierrot slip out last night?'

'Who told you he slipped out?'

'The concierge on Avenue Carnot, who knows him well, saw him enter the building and come out a quarter of an hour later.'

The owner was silent for a good moment, thinking about how best to react. He, too, was at the mercy of the police. 'Tell me first what happened to Lulu.'

'She was murdered.'

'Not by Pierrot!' he retorted with conviction.

'I didn't say it was by Pierrot.'

'So what do you want with him?'

'I need some information. You claim he was working here last night?'

'I'm not claiming anything. It's the truth. At seven o'clock, he was up there playing the saxophone.'

With his eyes, he indicated the balcony.

'But he slipped out about nine?'

'He had a phone call. It was twenty past nine.'

'Was it from Lulu?'

'I have no idea. It's quite likely.'

'I know,' the woman said. 'I was near the phone.'

The phone was not in a booth, but in a recess in the wall near the door to the toilets.

'He said to her, "I'll be right there." Then he turned to me. "Mélanie, I have to go over there." I asked him, "Is something wrong?" And he said, "It looks that way." Then he went up to talk to the other musicians and rushed out.'

'What time did he get back?'

This time, the man answered.

'Just before eleven.'

'Did he seem agitated?'

'I didn't notice anything. He apologized for his absence and went back to his place. He played until one in the morning. Then, as usual after closing, he had a drink with us. If he'd known that Lulu was dead, he wouldn't have had the guts. He was crazy about her. He always has been. I told him a hundred times, "You're wrong, Pierrot! You have to take women for what they are, and—"'

'Thanks very much!' his companion interrupted him curtly.

'It's not the same thing.'

'Wasn't Lulu in love with him?'

'Of course she was.'

'Did she have someone else?'

'A saxophone player couldn't have afforded an apartment in the Étoile area.'

'Do you know who it was?'

'She never told me, and nor did Pierrot. All I know is that her life changed after her operation.'

'What operation?'

'Two years ago, she was very ill. She was still living around here at the time.'

'Was she on the game?'

The man shrugged. 'What else can a girl do around here?'

'Carry on.'

'She was taken to hospital, and when Pierrot came back from visiting her, he said there was no hope. It was something in her head, I don't know what. Then, after two days, she was moved to another hospital, on the Left Bank. She had some kind of operation and recovered in a few weeks. Only, she didn't come back here, except to visit.'

'Did she immediately move to Avenue Carnot?'

'Do you remember?' the owner asked his wife.

'Yes, I do. First, she had an apartment in Rue La Fayette.'

When Janvier returned to Quai des Orfèvres, at about three, he knew no more than that. Maigret was still in his office, in his shirt-sleeves because the room was over-heated, and the air was blue with pipe smoke.

'Sit down. Tell me.'

Janvier recounted what he had done and what he had learned.

'I've asked for a watch to be kept on the railway stations,' Maigret said when he had finished. 'So far, Pierrot hasn't tried to take a train.'

He showed him a police record sheet containing both a full-face photograph and a profile photograph of a man who didn't look thirty, but a lot younger.

'Is that him?'

'Yes. At the age of twenty, he was arrested for the first time for aggravated assault during a fight in a bar in Avenue de Flandre. A year and a half later he was suspected of being an accessory in a theft committed by a girl he lived with, but it was never proved. At the age of twenty-four he was arrested one last time for vagrancy. He wasn't working at that time, just living off the immoral earnings of a girl named Ernestine. Since then, nothing. I've had his description circulated to the whole force. Is Janin still watching the hotel?'

'Yes. I thought it was wise.'

'You did the right thing. I don't think he'll be coming back any time soon, but we can't take the risk. Only, I need Janin. I'll send young Lapointe to replace him. You see, I'd be surprised if Pierrot tried to leave Paris. He's spent all his life in a neighbourhood he knows like the back of his hand, where it's easy for him to disappear. Janin knows his way around that neighbourhood better than we do. Call Lapointe.'

Lapointe listened to his instructions and rushed out with as much zeal as if the whole investigation depended on him.

'I also have the file on Louise Filon. Between the ages of fifteen and twenty-four she was picked up more than a hundred times in raids, taken to the cells, examined, put under observation and, most of the time, released after a few days. That's all,' Maigret sighed, knocking his pipe on his heel to empty it. 'Or rather, it isn't absolutely all, but the rest is vaguer.'

He might have been talking to himself, putting his thoughts in order, but Janvier was nevertheless flattered to be made party to them.

'Somewhere, there's a man who set Lulu up in that apartment on Avenue Carnot. It immediately struck me as odd this morning, a girl like her living in a building like that. You see what I mean?'

'Yes.'

It wasn't the kind of building where kept women usually lived. It wasn't even the kind of area. That building on Avenue Carnot oozed comfort and respectability, and it was surprising that the owner or manager should have agreed to let an apartment to a prostitute.

'My first thought was that the reason her lover set her up there was to have her close at hand. Now apparently, if the concierge isn't lying, Lulu didn't have any other visitors apart from Pierrot. She didn't go out regularly either, and she sometimes stayed at home for a whole week.'

'I'm starting to understand.'

'To understand what?'

Janvier turned red.

'I don't know,' he said.

'I don't know either. I'm just speculating. The man's slippers and dressing gown found in the wardrobe certainly don't belong to the saxophone player. At the shirt maker's in Rue de Rivoli they can't say who bought the dressing gown. They have hundreds of customers and don't keep records of names for cash purchases. As for the bootmaker, he's an old eccentric who claims he doesn't have time to look at his books today but promises he will one of these days. The fact remains that someone other than Pierrot was in the habit of going to see Louise Filon and was intimate enough with her to put on a dressing gown and slippers. If the concierge never saw him . . .'

'He must live in the building?'

'That's the most logical explanation.'

'Do you have a list of tenants?'

'Lucas phoned it to me earlier.'

Janvier was wondering why the chief had that grumpy air of his, as if there was something about this business he didn't like.

'What you told me about Lulu's illness and operation might be a clue, and in that case . . .'

He took time to light his pipe, bent over the list of names that was on his desk.

'You know who lives just above her apartment? Professor Gouin, the surgeon, who happens to be the greatest brain specialist around.'

Janvier's reaction was:

'Is he married?'

'Of course he's married, and his wife lives with him.'

'What are you going to do?'

'First of all, have a conversation with the concierge. Even if she didn't lie to me this morning, she certainly didn't tell me the whole truth. I might also pay a visit to Madame Brault, who may also know more than she's telling.'

'What shall I do?'

'Stay here. When Janin phones, ask him to start looking for Pierrot locally. Make sure he has a photograph with him.'

It was five o'clock, and already dark in the streets, by the time Maigret crossed the city in a police car. That morning, while his wife was looking through the window to see how people were dressed, he had had a curious thought. He had told himself that this day answered exactly to the image you have of a 'working day'. Those two words had come into his head for no reason, the way you remember the chorus of a song. It was a day when you couldn't imagine people being outside for their own pleasure, or even that they could find pleasure anywhere, a day when you were in a hurry, when you gritted your teeth and did what you had to do, trudging along in the rain, diving into Métro stations, into department stores, into offices, with nothing but dampness and greyness around you.

That was how he, too, had worked; his office was over-heated, and it was without any enthusiasm that he was once again on his way to Avenue Carnot, to a big stone building devoid of charm. Good old Lucas was still there, in the third-floor apartment, and from below Maigret caught a glimpse of him pulling the curtain aside and looking out gloomily into the street.

The concierge was sitting at the round table in her lodge, busy mending sheets. With her glasses on, she looked older. It was hot here, too, and very calm, the only sounds the ticking of an old clock and the hissing of the gas stove in the kitchen.

'Don't get up. I've come to have a chat with you.'

'Are you sure now she was murdered?' she asked as he took off his coat and sat down opposite her in a familiar manner.

'Unless someone took the gun off her after she died, which seems unlikely. The cleaning lady was only alone there for a few minutes, and I'm pretty sure she didn't take anything away with her when she left. Obviously, I didn't search her thoroughly. What are you thinking about, Madame Cornet?'

'Me? Nothing in particular. That poor girl.'

'Are you sure this morning you told me everything you know?'

He saw her turn red and bow her head lower over her sewing. A moment passed before she said, 'Why do you ask me that?'

'Because I have the impression you know the man who set Louise Filon up in this building. Was it you who let the apartment?'

'No, it was the manager.'

'I'll go and see him. He'll probably know more about it. I also think I'll go up to the fourth floor. There are some things I need to ask there.'

This time, she looked up abruptly.

'The fourth floor?'

'That is Professor Gouin's apartment, isn't it? If I understand correctly, he and his wife occupy the whole floor.'

'That's right.'

She had pulled herself together.

'I can at least ask them if they heard anything last night,'
he went on. 'Were they at home?'

'Madame Gouin was.'

'All day?'

'Yes. Her sister came to see her and stayed until half past
eleven.'

'What about the professor?'

'He left for the hospital about eight.'

'When did he get back?'

'At about a quarter past eleven. Just before his sister-
in-law left.'

'Does he often go to the hospital in the evening?'

'No, not often. Only when there's an emergency.'

'Is he at home now?'

'No. He almost never gets back before dinnertime. He
has an office in the apartment but he never sees patients
there, except in exceptional cases.'

'Then I'll go up and question his wife.'

She let him stand and walk to the chair on which he had
put his coat. He was about to open the door when she said
in a low voice:

'Monsieur Maigret!'

He had rather been expecting it and turned with a slight
smile. As she was searching for her words, with an almost
imploring look on her face, he said:

'Is it him?'

She misunderstood. 'You don't mean it's the professor who . . . ?'

'No, that's not what I mean. What I'm almost sure of, though, is that it was Professor Gouin who set Louise Filon up in this building.'

She nodded reluctantly.

'Why didn't you tell me?'

'You didn't ask.'

'I asked you if you knew the man who—'

'No. You asked me if I ever saw anyone go upstairs apart from the musician.'

It was pointless to argue.

'Did the professor ask you to keep quiet?'

'No. He doesn't care.'

'How do you know?'

'Because he doesn't hide.'

'Then why didn't you tell me—'

'I don't know. I didn't see any point in dragging him into it. He saved my son. He operated on him for free and treated him for more than two years.'

'Where is your son?'

'In the army. In Indochina.'

'Does Madame Gouin know?'

'Yes. She isn't jealous. She's used to it.'

'In other words, the whole building knows that Lulu was the professor's mistress?'

'If any of them don't know, it's because they don't want to know. In a place like this, tenants mind their own business. He often went down to the third floor in his pyjamas and dressing gown.'

'What kind of man is he?'

'Don't you know him?'

She was looking at Maigret with an air of disappointment. He had often seen Gouin's photograph in the newspapers but had never had the opportunity to meet him personally.

'He must be about sixty, isn't he?'

'Sixty-two, but he doesn't look it. Besides, for men like him, age doesn't matter.'

Maigret vaguely remembered a powerful face with a large nose, a strong chin, but cheeks that were already sagging and bags under the eyes. It was amusing to see the concierge talk about him with the same enthusiasm as a girl from the Conservatoire talking about her teacher.

'You don't know if he saw her last night before leaving for the hospital?'

'I told you it was only eight, and the young man came later.'

The only thing that concerned her was to place Gouin beyond suspicion.

'And after he got back?'

She was visibly searching for the best answer to give.

'Definitely not.'

'Why?'

'Because his sister-in-law came down a few minutes after he went up.'

'You think he saw his sister-in-law?'

'I assume she waited to see him before she left.'

'You're defending him quite fervently, Madame Cornet.'

'I'm simply telling the truth.'

'Since Madame Gouin knows about it, there's no reason I shouldn't see her.'

'Do you think that's tactful?'

'Maybe not. You're right.'

Nevertheless, he headed for the door.

'Where are you going?'

'Upstairs. I'll leave the door ajar, and when the professor gets back I'll ask to have a word with him.'

'If you really must.'

'Thank you.'

He liked her. Once the door was closed, he turned to look at her through the window. She had got to her feet and, on seeing him, seemed to think better of having stood up so quickly. She headed for the kitchen, as if she had something urgent to do there, but he was convinced it wasn't the kitchen she had been planning to rush to, but rather the side table by the window, where the telephone was.

3.

'Where did you find it?' Maigret asked Lucas.

'On the highest shelf of the cupboard in the kitchen.'

It was a white cardboard shoe box, and Lucas had left on the side table the red string that had been around it when he discovered it. Its contents reminded Maigret of other 'treasures' that he had seen so often in the country or among poor people: a marriage licence, a few yellowed letters, sometimes a receipt from a pawnshop, not always in a box but in a soup tureen from the best dinner set or in a fruit bowl.

Louise Filon's treasure wasn't so different. It didn't include a marriage licence, but part of a birth certificate issued by the town hall of the eighteenth arrondissement, stating that Louise Marie Joséphine Filon was born in Paris, daughter of Louis Filon, slaughterhouse worker, living in Rue de Cambrai, near the La Villette abattoir, and of Philippine Le Flem, laundress.

It was probably the mother who appeared in a photograph taken by a local photographer. The traditional backdrop showed a park with a balustrade in the foreground. The woman, who must have been about thirty when the photograph was taken, had been incapable of smiling to order and was staring straight ahead. She had presumably had other children apart from Louise, because her body was already shapeless, her breasts empty in her blouse.

Lucas had sat down in the armchair he had been occupying before going to open the door to Maigret. The latter had been unable to stop himself smiling as he came in, because near the ashtray, in which was a burning cigarette, lay one of Lulu's cheap novels: the sergeant must have grabbed it out of boredom and had already read almost half of it.

'She died,' Lucas said, pointing to the photograph. 'Seven years ago.'

He handed his chief a press cutting from the births, deaths and marriages column, which listed the people who had died that day, among them Philippine Filon, née Le Flem.

The two men had left the door ajar, and Maigret was listening out for the noise of the lift. The only time it had been in operation, it had stopped on the second floor.

'What about her father?'

'Just this letter.'

It was written in pencil, on cheap paper, and the handwriting was that of someone who hadn't had much schooling.

Dear Louise,

This is just to tell you that I'm in hospital again and I'm very unhappy. Maybe you'll be kind enough to send me a bit of money so that I can buy tobacco. They say eating makes me sick and they're letting me die of hunger. I'm sending this letter to the bar where someone who is here claims he saw you. I suppose they know you there. I won't make old bones.

Your father

In the corner was the name of a hospital in Béziers in the Hérault. The letter was undated, so there was no way of knowing when it had been written, probably two or three years earlier, to judge by how much the paper had yellowed.

Had Louise Filon received other letters? Why had she only kept this one? Was it because her father had died soon afterwards?

'Make inquiries in Béziers.'

'All right, chief.'

Maigret didn't see any other letters, just photographs, most taken at fairgrounds, some showing Louise on her own, others with Pierrot. There were also some identity photographs of the young woman taken with automatic cameras.

The rest consisted of trifling objects, also won at the fair: an earthenware dog, an ashtray, a drawn glass elephant, even paper flowers.

It would have been normal to unearth a treasure like this one somewhere in the area of Barbès or Boulevard de La Chapelle. Here, in an apartment on Avenue Carnot, the cardboard box took on an almost tragic aspect.

'Anything else?'

Just as Lucas was about to reply, the phone rang, making them both jump. Maigret hastened to pick up the receiver.

'Hello?' he said.

'Is Monsieur Maigret there?'

The voice was a woman's.

'Speaking.'

'I'm sorry to disturb you. I phoned your office, and they told me you were probably here, or that you would drop by. This is Madame Gouin speaking.'

'I'm listening.'

'May I come down and have a brief word with you?'

'Wouldn't it be easier if I came upstairs?'

The voice was firm. It remained so now as the reply came:

'I'd rather come down, to avoid my husband finding you in our apartment when he gets home.'

'As you wish.'

'I'll be right there.'

Maigret had time to whisper to Lucas:

'The wife of Professor Gouin, who lives upstairs.'

A few moments later, they heard footsteps on the stairs, then someone coming through the first door, which had been left open, and closing it behind her. Then there was a knock at the door communicating with the entrance hall, which had remained ajar, and Maigret stepped forwards.

'Come in, madame,' he said.

She did so naturally, as she might have come into any apartment, and, without looking round the room, her gaze immediately settled on Maigret.

'Let me introduce Sergeant Lucas. If you'd like to sit down . . .'

'Thank you.'

She was tall and quite sturdy, without being fat. Gouin was sixty-two, but she was probably forty-five and seemed no older.

48

'I assume you were rather expecting my phone call?' she said with a hint of a smile.

'Did the concierge tell you?'

She hesitated for a moment, without taking her eyes off him, and her smile intensified.

'Yes, she did. She just phoned me.'

'So you knew I was here. The reason you called my office was to make your coming to see me appear spontaneous.'

She barely blushed and lost nothing of her self-confidence. 'I should have suspected you would guess. I would have got in touch with you in any case, believe me. I've been meaning to talk to you since this morning, when I found out what happened here.'

'Why didn't you do so?'

'Perhaps because I'd rather my husband wasn't mixed up in this business.'

Maigret had not taken his eyes off her. He had noticed that she hadn't even glanced at her surroundings, that she had shown no curiosity.

'When were you last here, madame?'

This time, again, there was a slight blush on her cheeks, but she continued to play the game well.

'So you know that, too? Though I can't see who could have told you. Not even Madame Cornet.'

She thought it over and soon found the answer to her own question.

'I suppose I haven't behaved like someone coming into an apartment for the first time, especially an apartment where a murder has been committed?'

Lucas was sitting now on the sofa, almost in the place that Louise Filon's body had been occupying that morning. Madame Gouin had settled into an armchair, and Maigret remained standing, his back to the fireplace, in which there were only fake logs.

'Anyway, I'll answer you. One night, seven or eight months ago, the girl who lived here called me in a panic because my husband had just had a blackout. It was his heart.'

'Was he in the bedroom?'

'Yes. I came down and gave him first aid.'

'You've studied medicine?'

'Before our marriage, I was a nurse.'

Ever since she had come in, Maigret had been wondering what her background was, but had been unable to figure it out for himself. Now he better understood that self-confidence of hers.

'Carry on.'

'That's about it. I was going to phone a doctor who's a friend of ours when Étienne came round and forbade me to call anybody.'

'Was he surprised to find you at his bedside?'

'No. He's always told me everything. He's never hidden anything from me. That night, he came back upstairs with me and finally fell asleep peacefully.'

'Was it his first attack?'

'He'd had another one three years earlier, but that was milder.'

She was still calm and self-controlled, just as you imagined her in her nurse's uniform by a patient's bedside. Of the two men, Lucas was the more surprised, as he wasn't yet familiar with the situation and couldn't understand how a woman could speak so calmly about her husband's mistress.

'Why did you want to speak to me this evening?' Maigret asked.

'The concierge told me you intended to talk to my husband. I wondered if it wasn't possible to avoid that, if a conversation with me wouldn't provide you with the same information. Do you know the professor?'

'Only by reputation.'

'He's an extraordinary man. You find only a few like him in a generation.'

Maigret nodded.

'He devotes his whole life to his work, which he regards as a true vocation. Apart from his classes and his duties at the Cochin hospital, he sometimes performs three or four operations on the same day, and I'm sure you know these are extremely difficult operations. Is it any surprise that I should make every effort to spare him any worries?'

'Have you seen your husband since the death of Louise Filon?'

'He came home for lunch. This morning, when he left, there were already comings and goings in this apartment, but we didn't know anything.'

'How did he seem at lunch?'

'It was a blow to him.'

'Did he love her?'

She looked at him for a moment without replying. Then she glanced at Lucas, whose presence she seemed to find disagreeable.

'I think, Monsieur Maigret, from what I know of you, that you're a man capable of understanding. It's precisely because other people wouldn't understand that I'd like to avoid this story getting out. The professor is a man who shouldn't be the object of gossip, and his activities are too valuable to everyone to risk undermining them by pointless worries.'

In spite of himself, Maigret glanced at the place Lulu's body had occupied that morning, and it was a kind of comment on the words 'pointless worries'.

'Do you mind if I try to give you some idea of his character?'

'Not at all.'

'You probably know that he was born into a family of poor peasants in the Cévennes.'

'I knew he came from a peasant family.'

'What he's become, he's become by force of will. It wouldn't be too much of an exaggeration to say that he was never a child, or a young man. You understand what I mean?'

'Very well.'

'He's a kind of force of nature. Even though I'm his wife, I don't mind saying that he's a man of genius, because others have said it before me and continue to say it.'

Maigret was still nodding.

'People in general have a strange attitude to geniuses. They're prepared to admit that they're different from other people as far as intelligence and professional activities are concerned. Any patient of his thinks it's only natural that Gouin should get up at two o'clock in the morning for an emergency operation that only he can perform, and that by nine o'clock he should be at the hospital, dealing with other patients. But those same patients would be shocked to learn that he's different from them in other ways, too.'

Maigret could guess what was coming next but he preferred to let her talk. She did so with persuasive calm.

'Étienne has never bothered with the little pleasures of life. He has no real friends. I don't remember him ever taking a proper holiday. His expenditure of energy is incredible. The only way he's ever found to relax is with women.'

She glanced at Lucas, then turned again to Maigret.

'I hope I'm not shocking you?'

'Not at all.'

'Do you understand what I'm saying? He's not the kind of man to flirt with women. He wouldn't have the patience, or the inclination. What he asks of them is some quick relief, and I don't think he's ever been in love in his life.'

'Not even with you?'

'I've often wondered that. I really don't know. We've been married for twenty-two years. Before our marriage he was a bachelor and lived with an old housekeeper.'

'In this building?'

'Yes. He just happened to rent our apartment when he was thirty, and it's never occurred to him to move, not even when he was appointed to Cochin, which is on the other side of the city.'

'Were you in his department?'

'Yes. I imagine I can speak to you frankly?'

It was still the presence of Lucas that embarrassed her, and Lucas, who sensed it, was ill at ease and kept crossing and uncrossing his short legs.

'For months, he paid no attention to me. I knew, as did the whole hospital, that most of the nurses had their turn eventually, and that it never led to anything. By the next day he always seemed to have forgotten. One night when I was on duty, and we had to wait for the result of an operation that had lasted three hours, he had me, without a word.'

'Did you love him?'

'I think I did. I certainly admired him. A few days later, I was surprised when he asked me out to lunch with him in a restaurant on Faubourg Saint-Jacques. He asked me if I was married. He hadn't shown any interest in that before then. Then he asked me what my parents did, and I told him my father was a fisherman in Brittany. Am I boring you?'

'Not at all.'

'I really would like you to understand.'

'Aren't you afraid he'll come back and be surprised not to find you upstairs?'

'Before coming down, I phoned the Saint-Joseph Clinic, where he's operating right now, and I know he won't get home until half past seven.'

It was 6.15 now.

'What was I saying? Oh, yes. We had lunch together, and he wanted to know what my father did. This is where it gets harder. Especially as I wouldn't want you to get the wrong idea. It reassured him to know that I came from a similar family to his. What nobody knows is that he's terribly shy, I was going to say unhealthily shy, but only with people who belong to a different social class. I assume that's why he was still unmarried at the age of forty and why he'd never moved in what's called society. All the girls he had were common.'

'I understand.'

'I wonder if, with someone else, he could have . . .'

She blushed as she said these words, thus giving them a specific meaning.

'He got used to me, even though he never stopped behaving with the others the way he always had. Then, one fine day, he asked me, almost absent-mindedly, if I wanted to marry him. That's our whole story. I came to live here. I've kept house for him.'

'Did the housekeeper leave?'

'A week after we were married. Needless to say, I'm not jealous. That would be ridiculous on my part.'

Maigret couldn't remember ever looking at anyone so intensely as he was looking at this woman. She sensed it and wasn't intimidated; on the contrary, she appeared to understand the interest he had in her.

She was trying to say everything, to leave no character trait of her great man in the shadows.

'He continued sleeping with the nurses, with his successive assistants, in fact with any girl he came across who wasn't likely to complicate his life. Perhaps that's the main point. He would never accept an affair that would make him waste time he considers he owes to his work.'

'What about Lulu?'

'You already know she was called Lulu? I'm getting there. It's as simple as the rest, you'll see. Do you mind if I get a glass of water?'

Lucas tried to stand up, but she had already got to the kitchen, where they heard the tap running. When she sat down again, her lips were moist, and there was a drop of liquid on her chin.

She wasn't pretty in the usual sense of the word, nor was she beautiful, in spite of her regular features. But she was pleasant to look at. There was a kind of calming influence in her. Maigret would have liked to be treated by her if he was sick. And she was also the kind of woman you could have lunch or dinner with somewhere without worrying about keeping up the conversation. A friend, in other words, someone who understood everything, who was never surprised or shocked or offended by anything.

'I suppose you know how old he is?'

'Sixty-two.'

'Yes. Mind you, he's lost none of his vigour. And I use the word in all its senses. All the same, I think all men, at a certain age, are terrified at the thought of seeing their virility diminish.'

Realizing as she spoke that Maigret was over fifty, she stammered:

'Oh, I'm sorry . . .'

'It's all right.'

It was the first time they had smiled at each other.

'I suppose it's the same with other men. I have no idea. The fact is, Étienne has been even more determined than ever in his sexual activities. Haven't I shocked you yet?'

'Not yet.'

'About two years ago, he had a young patient, Louise Filon, whose life he miraculously saved. I assume you already know all about her previous life? She comes from as far down the social ladder as it's possible to come, and that's probably what interested my husband.'

Maigret nodded, because everything she said sounded true, with all the simplicity of a police report.

'It must have started at the hospital, when she was convalescing. Then he set her up in an apartment in Rue La Fayette, after mentioning it to me casually. He didn't go into details. He's always been reticent about such things. All at once, in the course of a meal, he told me what he'd done, or what he was intending to do. I didn't ask him any questions. And then we didn't speak about it any more.'

'Was it you who suggested she come and live in this building?'

It seemed to please her that Maigret had guessed.

'For you to understand, I need to go into more detail. I'm sorry to be taking so long. But it all hangs together. Étienne used to drive his car himself. A few years ago, four years to be precise, he had a small accident on Place de la Concorde. He knocked down a woman who was passing. Luckily, she escaped with bruises. All the same, he was upset. For a few months, we had a chauffeur, but he never got used to it. It shocked him that a man in the prime of life should have nothing better to do than wait for him for hours at the kerb. I offered to drive him, but that wasn't practical either, so he got into the habit of using taxis. The car stayed in the garage for several months, and we ended up selling it. In the morning, it's always the same taxi driver who comes to pick him up and drives him around for part of the day. It's quite a long way from here to Faubourg Saint-Jacques. He has patients at Neuilly, too, and often in other hospitals around the city. Going to Rue La Fayette on top of all that . . .'

Maigret was still nodding, while Lucas seemed to be dozing off.

'As luck would have it, an apartment became free in this building.'

'One moment. Did your husband often spend the night in Rue La Fayette?'

'Only part of the night. He always tried to be here in the morning for when his assistant, who's also his secretary, gets here.' She gave a little laugh. 'In a way, it was all because of these domestic complications. I asked him if there was any reason he shouldn't set up the girl here.'

'You knew who she was?'

'I knew everything about her, including the fact that she had a boyfriend named Pierrot.'

'Did he also know that?'

'Yes. He wasn't jealous. He probably wouldn't have liked to find him with Lulu, but, as long as it happened when he wasn't there . . .'

'Carry on. He agreed to the idea. What about her?'

'Apparently, she resisted for a while.'

'What, in your opinion, were Louise Filon's feelings for the professor?'

Maigret was starting automatically to talk in the same tone as Madame Gouin about this man he had never seen and who seemed almost present in the room.

'Would you like me to be frank?'

'Please.'

'First of all, like all the women who come near him, she fell under his spell. You're going to think it's a strange kind of pride on my part, but even though he isn't what people call handsome and he's far from young, I know few women who have resisted him. Women instinctively feel his strength and . . .'

This time, she couldn't find the words she was looking for.

'Anyway, it's a fact, and I don't think the women you question will contradict me. This girl was just like the others. What's more, he saved her life and treated her in a way she wasn't used to being treated.'

All clear and logical so far.

'To be perfectly honest, I'm convinced the question of money played its part. If not money exactly, at least the prospect of a certain security, a life devoid of worries.'

'Did she ever talk about leaving him for her boyfriend?'

'Not as far as I know.'

'Did you ever see the man?'

'I passed him once at the front entrance.'

'Did he come here often?'

'Generally not. She'd meet him in the afternoon some-where or other. On rare occasions, he came to see her.'

'Did your husband know that?'

'It's possible.'

'Would he have been displeased?'

'Perhaps, though not out of jealousy. It's hard to explain.'

'Was your husband very fond of the girl?'

'She owed him everything. He was almost her creator, since without him, she would have died. Maybe he was thinking of the day when he wouldn't have any others? Plus, with her, although this is only a supposition, he felt no shame.'

'And with you?'

She stared at the carpet for a moment. 'I'm a woman, after all.'

He almost retorted: 'While she was nothing!'

Because that was clearly what she thought. Perhaps it was what the professor thought, too?

He preferred not to say it. All three were silent for a moment. Outside, the rain was still falling noiselessly. Lights had come on in the building opposite, and a shadow was moving behind the cream-coloured curtains of an apartment.

'Tell me about last night,' Maigret said at last. He indicated his pipe, which he had just filled. 'Do you mind?'

'Not at all.'

So far, he had been so interested in Madame Gouin that he had not thought about smoking.

'What would you like me to tell you?'

'First, a detail. Was your husband in the habit of sleeping in her apartment?'

'It was extremely rare. Upstairs, we occupy the whole floor. On the left is what we call the apartment. On the right, my husband has his bedroom and bathroom, a library, another room where even the floor is piled high with scientific pamphlets, and finally his office and his secretary's office.'

'So you sleep separately?'

'We always have. Our rooms are only separated by a boudoir.'

'May I ask you an indiscreet question?'

'You're perfectly entitled.'

'Do you still have marital relations with your husband?'

She looked once again at poor Lucas, who was feeling superfluous and didn't know what to do with himself.

'Not often.'

'In other words, almost never?'

'That's right.'

'How long has that been the case?'

'Some years.'

'Do you miss it?'

Unembarrassed, she smiled and nodded.

'You're asking me to tell all, and I'm ready to answer you as frankly as possible. Let's say I miss it a little.'

'Do you ever let on to him about that?'

'Certainly not.'

'Do you have a lover?'

'The idea's never even crossed my mind.' She paused, and looked straight at him. 'Do you believe me?'

'Yes.'

'I'm grateful. People don't always accept the truth. When you're the companion of a man like Gouin, you're prepared to make certain sacrifices.'

'So he would go downstairs to see her and come back up again?'

'Yes.'

'Is that what he did last night?'

'No. It didn't happen every day. Sometimes, almost a week would go by with him just dropping in on her for a few minutes. It depended on his work. I suppose it also depended on the opportunities he found elsewhere.'

'You mean he continued having relations with other women?'

'The kind of relations I described to you.'

'And yesterday?'

'He saw her for a few minutes after dinner. I know that because he didn't take the lift when he left, which is a sign.'

'How can you be sure he only stayed a few minutes?'

'Because I heard him come out of this apartment and summon the lift.'

'Were you listening out for him?'

'You're terrible, Monsieur Maigret. I was listening out for him, yes, as I always did, not out of jealousy, but . . . How can I explain without appearing pretentious? Because I considered it my duty in a way to protect him, to know everything he did, where he was, to follow him in my thoughts.'

'What time was it?'

'About eight. We'd eaten quickly, because he was supposed to spend the evening at Cochin. He was worried about the consequences of an operation he had performed in the afternoon and wanted to stay within easy reach of the patient.'

'So he spent a few minutes in her apartment, then took the lift?'

'Yes. His assistant, Mademoiselle Decaux, was waiting for him downstairs, as she usually does when he goes back in the evening to the hospital. She lives not far from here, in Rue des Acacias, and they always travel together.'

'Does she also . . . ?' he asked, giving an obvious meaning to these words.

'Yes, on occasion. Does that strike you as monstrous?'

'No.'

'Where was I? My sister arrived at about half past eight.'

'Does she live in Paris?'

'On Boulevard Saint-Michel, opposite the École des Mines. Antoinette is five years older than me and has never married. She works in a municipal library and is the very model of a spinster.'

'Does she know about your husband's life?'

'She doesn't know everything. But from what she's discovered, she thoroughly hates and despises him.'

'So they don't get on?'

'She never even talks to him. My sister is still a devout Catholic, and for her Gouin is the devil incarnate.'

'And how does he treat her?'

'He ignores her. She doesn't come here very often, and only when I'm alone in the apartment.'

'So she avoids him?'

'As much as possible.'

'And yet yesterday . . .'

'I see the concierge told you everything. It's true they met last night. I didn't expect my husband back before midnight at the earliest. My sister and I were chatting.'

'What about?'

'This and that.'

'Did you talk about Lulu?'

'I don't think so.'

'Aren't you sure?'

'Actually, I am. I don't know why I gave that evasive answer. As a matter of fact, we talked about our parents.'

'Are they dead?'

'My mother's dead, but my father's still alive, in Finistère. We have other sisters there. There were eight of us, six girls and two boys.'

'Do any of them live in Paris?'

'Only Antoinette and I. At half past eleven, perhaps a little earlier, we were surprised to hear the door open and see Étienne come in. He simply nodded. Antoinette said goodbye and left almost immediately.'

'Did your husband go downstairs?'

'No. He was tired and worried about his patient, whose condition wasn't as satisfactory as he would have liked.'

'I assume he has a key to this apartment?'

'Of course.'

'During the evening, did anything unusual happen? Did your sister and you hear any noise?'

'In these old stone buildings, you can't hear anything from one apartment to another, let alone one floor to another.'

She looked at the time on her wristwatch and grew nervous.

'I'm so sorry, but I'm going to have to go back upstairs. Étienne may be back any minute now. Do you have any other questions to ask me?'

'I can't think of any for the moment.'

'Do you think it'll be possible for you to avoid questioning him?'

'I can't promise anything, but I'll only bother your husband if I consider it indispensable.'

'What do you think now?'

'Now, I don't consider it indispensable.'

She stood up and held out her hand, as a man would have done, without taking her eyes off him. 'I'm very grateful, Monsieur Maigret.'

As she was turning, her gaze fell on the cardboard box and the photographs, but Maigret couldn't see the expression on her face.

'I'm at home all day. You can come and see me when my husband isn't in. But in saying that, I'm sure you'll understand it isn't a demand, but a request.'

'It never occurred to me to think otherwise.'

'Thank you.'

She went out, closing the two doors behind her, while little Lucas looked at Maigret with the air of a man who has just received a blow on the head. He was so afraid of saying something stupid that he kept silent, observing Maigret's face in the hope of reading on it what he must be thinking.

4.

Oddly, in the car taking him back to the Police Judiciaire, it wasn't Professor Gouin, or his wife, that Maigret was thinking about, but, almost unwittingly, Louise Filon: before leaving, he had slipped her fairground photographs into his wallet.

Even in those photographs, taken as they were on evenings when she should have been in a lively mood, there was no gaiety in her face. Maigret had known lots of women like her, born in identical surroundings, who had had a more or less identical childhood and life. Some had a vulgar, boisterous gaiety about them that could give way without transition to tears or rebellion. Others, like Désirée Brault, became hard and cynical, especially with age.

It was hard to define the expression he found in Lulu's photographs, an expression she must have had in life. It wasn't sadness, but rather the sullen expression of a little girl who keeps to herself in the school playground and watches her schoolmates play.

He would have been hard put to explain in what way she had been attractive, but he sensed it and he had often, in spite of himself, questioned such girls more gently than others.

They were young and retained a certain freshness; in some respects, they seemed barely more than children, and yet they had been through a lot and there were too many disgusting images in their no longer sparkling eyes, while their bodies had the unhealthy charm of something that will wither, that is half withered already.

He imagined her in the hotel room in Rue Briquet, or in any room in the Barbès district, spending days on a bed, reading, sleeping or looking at the murky window. He imagined her in some café or other in the eighteenth arron-dissement, sitting for hours while someone like Pierrot played *belote* with three of his pals. He also imagined her in a dance hall, her face grave and almost inspired as she danced. He imagined her finally, standing on a street corner, watching the men in the shadows, without bothering to smile at them, and then leading them up the stairs of a rooming house, shouting out her name to the manageress.

She had lived for more than a year in the impressive stone building on Avenue Carnot, where the apartment seemed too big, too cold for her, and it was there that he found it hard to imagine her; it was face to face with a man like Étienne Gouin that he couldn't somehow see her.

Most of the lights were off in Quai des Orfèvres. He slowly climbed the stairs, where wet soles had left prints, and opened the door to his office. Janvier was waiting for him. It was the time of year when the contrast is most noticeable between the cold outside and the warmth of buildings, which seem overheated and where the blood immediately rushes to your head.

'Any news?'

The police machine was dealing with Pierre Eyraud. At the railway stations, inspectors were examining those trav-ellers whose description matched his. At the airports, too. The Hotel Agency were probably also on the trail, scouring the hotels and rooming houses of the eighteenth arrondissement.

In Rue Briquet, young Lapointe had been hanging about outside the Hôtel du Var since early afternoon. Now that night had fallen, prostitutes were prowling about the hotel.

As for Inspector Janin, the local man, he was indulging in a more personal kind of search . . . The north-east of Paris was a stone jungle in which a man can disappear for months, where often you don't hear about a crime until weeks after it has been committed; thousands of people, men and women, live outside the law, in a world where they find as many refuges and helping hands as they want and where the police occasionally cast a net and pick up someone they are looking for, quite by chance, but are more likely to rely on a telephone call from a jealous girl or an informer.

'Gastine-Renette called an hour ago.'

He was the ballistics expert.

'What did he say?'

'You'll have his written report tomorrow morning. The bullet that killed Louise Filon was fired from a 6.35 calibre automatic.'

What in the Police Judiciaire is called an amateur weapon. Real criminals, those who really have the intent to kill, use more serious weapons.

'Dr Paul also phoned. He'd like you to get in touch with him.' Janvier looked at his watch. It was just after 7.15. 'By now he's probably at the restaurant, La Pérouse, where he's guest of honour at a dinner.'

Maigret called the restaurant. A few moments later, the pathologist came on the line.

'I carried out a post-mortem on the girl you sent me. I may be mistaken, but I have the impression I've seen her before.'

'She was arrested several times.'

It couldn't have been Lulu's face, distorted by the gunshot, that the doctor thought he had recognized, but her body.

'Obviously the shot was fired at close range. It doesn't take an expert to see that. I reckon the distance was between 25 and 30 centimetres, no more than that.'

'I assume death was instantaneous.'

'As instantaneous as could be. The stomach still contained undigested food, including lobster.'

Maigret remembered seeing an empty lobster can in the waste bin in the kitchen.

'She drank white wine with her meal. Is that of any interest?'

Maigret did not yet know. At this stage of the investigation, it was impossible to say what might prove important.

'I discovered something else that may surprise you. Did you know the girl was pregnant?'

Maigret was indeed surprised, so surprised that for a moment he did not speak.

'How far gone?' he asked at last.

'About six weeks. She might not even have known. If she did know, she'd probably only recently found out.'

'I assume you're certain about this?'

'Absolutely. You'll get the technical details in my report.'

Maigret hung up and said to Janvier, who was standing waiting in front of the desk:

'She was pregnant.'

But Janvier, who knew only the broad outline of the case, was unimpressed by this.

'What shall we do with Lapointe?' he asked.

'That's a good point. We should send someone to take his place.'

'I have Lober, who has nothing in particular to do.'

'We should also relieve Lucas. There's probably no point, but I'd still like to have someone keeping an eye on the apartment.'

'If I can eat something first, I'll go. Is it OK to sleep there?'

'I don't see any reason why not.'

Maigret glanced at the latest editions of the newspapers. The photograph of Pierrot had not been published yet. It must have reached the editorial offices too late, but his complete description was given.

The police are looking for Louise Filon's boyfriend, a dance-hall musician named Pierre Eyraud, known as Pierrot, who was the last person to visit her last night.

Pierre Eyraud, who has served a number of prison sentences, has dropped out of sight. He is believed to be hiding in the La Chapelle district, which he knows well . . .

Maigret shrugged, stood up and hesitated before heading for the door.

'If there are any developments, can you be reached at home?'

He said yes. He had no reason to stay in the office. He had himself driven home in one of the cars, and, as usual, Madame Maigret opened the door to the apartment before he had turned the handle. She made no reference to the fact that he was late. Dinner was ready.

'I hope you didn't catch cold?'

'I don't think so.'

'You should take your shoes off.'

'My feet aren't wet.'

It was true. He hadn't walked all day. On a cabinet lay the same evening paper he had glanced through at the office. His wife knew all about it, then, but she did not ask him any questions.

She knew he wanted to go out again, because he hadn't taken off his tie as he almost always did. Once dinner was over, she watched her husband open the sideboard and pour himself a glass of sloe gin.

'Are you going out?'

Even a moment earlier, he hadn't been sure. To tell the truth, he had rather been expecting Professor Gouin to phone him. It was based on nothing specific. Wasn't Gouin thinking that the police would question him? Wasn't he surprised they weren't paying any attention to him, even though a lot of people knew about his relations with Lulu?

He called Louise Filon's apartment. Janvier had just settled in.

'Anything to report?'

'Nothing new, chief. I've let my wife know. It's nice and quiet here. I'm going to spend the night on the sofa, which is fantastic.'

'Do you know if the professor has come home?'

'Lucas told me he went up about half past seven. I haven't heard him go out.'

'Goodnight.'

Had Gouin guessed that his wife would talk to Maigret? Had she been capable of not letting on to him? What had they said to each other as they were having dinner? Presumably, once the meal was over, the professor was in the habit of retiring to his office.

Maigret poured himself another glass, which he drank standing by the sideboard, then walked over to the coat stand and took down his heavy overcoat.

'Take a scarf. Do you think you'll be out for long?'

'An hour or two.'

He had to walk as far as Boulevard Voltaire to find a taxi. He gave the driver the address of the Grelot. There was little bustle in the streets, except round Gare de l'Est and Gare du Nord. Gare du Nord always reminded Maigret of his early years in the police.

On Boulevard de La Chapelle, below the overhead Métro, the familiar shadowy figures were in their places, the same as every night, and although it was obvious what the women were doing there, what they were waiting for, it was less easy to define the reasons some men had to be there, doing nothing, in the cold and dark. They weren't all searching for a temporary companion. Nor did all of them have an appointment. There were men of all races and ages, who emerged from their holes at night like rats and ventured to the edges of their territory.

The neon sign of the Grelot cast a purple light on a section of the pavement, and from the taxi Maigret made out muted music, more like a rhythm accompanied by a muted shuffling. Two uniformed officers were standing on duty under a streetlamp a short distance away, and at the door there was a midget who seemed to be taking the air but who hurried inside when Maigret got out of the cab.

That is always the way in such places. No sooner had Maigret entered than two men pushed past him and hurried out, heading for the darkest depths of the neighbourhood.

At the bar, others turned their heads away as he passed them, in the hope of not being recognized, and as soon as his back was turned sped off in their turn.

The short, stocky owner came towards him. 'If it's Pierrot you're looking for, inspector . . .'

He was deliberately speaking loudly, underlining the word 'inspector' so that everyone in the room should know who he was. Here, too, the light was purple, and the customers sitting at the tables and in the booths could barely be made out, because only the dance-floor was lit, and the faces received only the reflected glow of the spotlights, making them look ghostly.

The music did not stop playing, or the couples dancing, but the conversations had ceased, and all eyes were turned to the massive figure of Maigret, who was looking for a free table.

'Would you like to sit down?'

'Yes.'

'This way, inspector . . .'

Saying this, the owner had the air of a fairground entertainer showing off in front of the painted canvas of his booth.

'What are you drinking? It's on the house.'

Maigret had expected that as he came in. He was used to it.

'A marc.'

'An old marc for Inspector Maigret!'

The four musicians were on their balcony, wearing black trousers and dark-red silk shirts with long puffed sleeves. They had found a way to replace Pierrot: someone was playing the saxophone, alternating with the accordion.

'Is it me you want to talk to?'

Maigret shook his head and pointed to the balcony.

'The musicians?'

'Whoever knows Pierrot best.'

'That'd be Louis, the accordion player. He's the one leading the band. They'll be taking a break in a quarter of an hour, and he can come and talk to you for a bit. I don't suppose you're in any hurry?'

Five or six more people, including one of the dancers, felt the need to go out for air. Ignoring them, Maigret looked calmly around him, and the people gradually resumed their conversations.

There were a certain number of prostitutes here, but they weren't on the lookout for clients. They had come to dance, most with their boyfriends, and they were absorbed in their dancing, which for them was a kind of sacred ritual. Some had their eyes closed, as if in ecstasy, others danced cheek to cheek with their partners but without trying to move their bodies closer.

There were also typists and shop girls in the room, who were only there for the music and the dancing, and you didn't see any onlookers, any couples out for a good time, as in most dance halls, getting a kick out of rubbing shoulders with the underworld.

There were only two or three dance halls like this left in all of Paris. Most of the people here were initiates, and they drank lemonade rather than alcohol.

From the balcony, the four musicians were looking imperturbably at Maigret, and it was impossible to guess what they were thinking. The accordion player was a handsome brown-haired man of about thirty who looked like a matinee idol and had long Spanish-style sideburns.

A man with a big pocket in his apron collected small change.

Couples remained on the dance-floor. There was another dance, a tango this time, for which the spotlights changed from purple to red, erasing the women's make-up, staining the musicians' shirts, and then at last the musicians put down their instruments, and the owner said a few words from below to the accordion player, whom he had called Louis.

Louis looked once again at Maigret's table and made up his mind to come down the ladder.

'You can sit down,' Maigret said.

'We start again in ten minutes.'

'That's all I need. What will you have?'

'Nothing.'

A silence followed. They were being watched from the other tables. There were more men crowding around the bar now. In some of the booths, there were only women, touching up their make-up.

Louis was the first to speak.

'You're making a big mistake,' he said in a rancorous tone.

'About Pierrot?'

'Pierrot didn't kill Lulu. But it's always the same!'

'Why has he run away?'

'He's no more stupid than anyone else. He knows he'll get the blame for it. Would you like to be arrested?'

'Is he your friend?'

'Yes, he's my friend. I probably know him better than anyone else.'

'Then maybe you know where he is.'

'If I did, I wouldn't tell you.'

'Do you know?'

'No. I haven't heard from him since we said goodbye last night. Have you read the papers?' Louis' voice was shaking with contained anger. 'People assume that, just because someone plays in a dance hall, he has to be some kind of tough guy. Maybe you think that, too?'

'No.'

'You see the tall fair-haired guy who plays the drums? Well, believe it or not, he's someone who graduated from high school and even spent a year at university. His parents are comfortably off. He's here because he loves it and he's getting married next week to a girl who's studying medicine. I'm married, too, if you really want to know, I have two children, my wife is expecting a third, and we live in a four-roomed apartment on Boulevard Voltaire.'

Maigret knew it was true. Louis was forgetting that the inspector knew that environment almost as well as he did.

'Why hasn't Pierrot married?' he nevertheless asked in a low voice.

'That's another story.'

'Didn't Lulu want to?'

'I didn't say that.'

'A few years ago, Pierrot was arrested as a pimp.'

'I know.'

'And?'

'Like I said, that's another story.'

'What story?'

'You still wouldn't understand. First of all, he was in care when he was a child. You know what that means?'

'Yes.'

'At the age of sixteen, they let him go, and he did what he could. In his place, I might have been worse than him. But I had parents like everyone else. I still have them.'

He was proud to be a man like any other, but at the same time he felt the need to defend those who found themselves on the other side of the tracks, and Maigret could not help smiling sympathetically.

'Why do you smile?'

'Because I know all this.'

'If you knew Pierrot, you wouldn't set all your informers on his tracks.'

'How do you know the police are after him?'

'The papers haven't made it all up. And you can already feel a stir in the neighbourhood. When you spot certain faces around, you know what that means.'

Louis didn't like the police and made no attempt to hide it.

'There was a time when Pierrot acted tough,' he went on.

'And wasn't he?'

'Will you believe me if I tell you he's soft-hearted, a romantic? Well, it's the truth.'

'Did he love Lulu?'

'Yes.'

'Did he meet her when she was on the game?'

'Yes.'

'And he let her carry on.'

'What else could he have done? You see, you don't understand!'

'Then he let her have a regular lover who kept her.'

'That's different.'

'Why?'

'Can you tell me what he had to offer her? Do you imagine he could have supported her with what he earns here?'

'You support your family, don't you?'

'Wrong! My wife's a dressmaker and works ten hours a day as well as looking after the kids. What you don't understand is that, when you're born around here, when you haven't known anything else . . .' He broke off. 'I only have four minutes left.'

The other musicians were still looking at them from the balcony, their faces expressionless.

'What I know is that he didn't kill her. And the only reason he didn't get her away from that doctor of hers—'

'So you know who Lulu's lover was?'

'What of it?'

'Was it Pierrot who told you?'

'Everyone knows it started at the hospital. All right, I'll tell you what Pierrot thought about it. She had a chance to get away from this once and for all, to have a steady life and not worry about the future. That's why he said nothing.'

'And Lulu?'

'Maybe she had her reasons.'

'What were they?'

'It's none of my business.'

'What kind of girl was she?'

Louis looked at the women around them with the air of saying she was no different from the others.

'She had a tough life,' he said, as if that explained everything. 'She wasn't happy down there.'

'Down there' clearly meant the distant Étoile neighbourhood, which, from here, seemed like another world.

'She came here from time to time to dance . . .'

'Did she seem unhappy?'

Louis shrugged. Did that word have a meaning in La Chapelle? Were there any truly happy women around them? Even the shop girls looked nostalgic as they danced and requested sad songs.

'We only have a minute. If you still need me after that, you'll have to wait half an hour.'

'When he got back from Avenue Carnot last night, did Pierrot say anything to you?'

'He apologized and said he'd had some important news, but didn't go into details.'

'Did he seem down?'

'He's always down.'

'Did you know that Lulu was pregnant?'

Louis stared at him, incredulous at first, then stunned and finally grave.

'Are you sure of that?'

'The pathologist who carried out the post-mortem can't have made a mistake.'

'How many months?'

'Six weeks.'

That made an impression on him, perhaps because he had children and his wife was expecting another. He turned to the waiter who was standing not far from them, trying to hear their conversation.

'Give me something to drink, Ernest. It doesn't matter what.'

He'd forgotten that the minute had passed. From the bar, the owner was watching them.

'I didn't expect that.'

'Neither did I,' Maigret added.

'I assume the professor's too old?'

'Men have fathered children at the age of eighty.'

'If what you say is true, it's one more reason why he couldn't have killed her.'

'Listen to me, Louis.'

The musician was still looking at Maigret with a certain suspicion, but he had lost his aggressiveness.

'You may hear from Pierrot. One way or another. I'm not asking you to give him up. Just to tell him that I'd like to talk to him, wherever he likes, whenever he likes. Have you got that?'

'And will you let him go?'

'I'm not saying I'll call off the search. All I can promise is that when he leaves me he'll be free.'

'What do you intend to ask him?'

'I don't know yet.'

'Do you still think he killed Lulu?'

'I don't think anything.'

'I doubt he'll get in touch with me.'

'But if he does . . .'

'I'll see he gets your message. Now, if you'll excuse me . . .'

Downing his drink, he climbed up to the balcony and secured the straps of the accordion around his waist and shoulders. The others didn't question him. He bent over them, but only to tell them the title of the piece they were going to play. The men at the bar examined the seated girls from a distance, looking for the ones they would ask to dance.

'Waiter!'

'There's nothing to pay. It's on the house.'

There was no point arguing. He stood up and headed for the door.

'Have you found out anything?'

There was irony in the owner's voice.

'Thanks for the marc.'

It was pointless looking for a taxi in the neighbourhood, and Maigret walked to Boulevard de La Chapelle, brushing aside the prostitutes who didn't know him and tried to approach him. Three hundred metres away were the lights of the Barbès intersection. It had stopped raining. The same fog as in the morning was starting to fall over the city, and the car lights were surrounded by haloes.

Rue Briquet was not far. He soon turned the corner and found Inspector Lober, who was almost the same age as he was but had never risen in rank, leaning against a wall and smoking a cigarette.

'Anything?'

'Lots of couples going in and out, but I didn't see him.'

Maigret felt like sending Lober home to bed. He could have telephoned Janvier and told him to go home, too. And called off the surveillance in the railway stations, because he was sure Pierrot wouldn't try to leave Paris. Only, he was obliged to follow routine. He couldn't afford to take any risks.

'Aren't you cold?'

Lober already smelled of rum. As long as the corner bistro remained open, he'd be fine. That was why he would stay an inspector all his life.

'Goodnight, my friend! If anything new crops up, phone me at home.'

It was eleven o'clock. The crowds were starting to emerge from the cinemas. On the pavements, couples were walking arm in arm, and women had their arms round their partners' waists; there were some who lingered in dark corners, embracing, while others ran to catch their bus.

Off the lighted boulevards, every sidestreet had its own arrangement, its own shadows, and every one also had, somewhere along its length, the yellowish signs of one or two hotels.

It was towards the lights that he walked. He went into a garishly lit bar at the Barbès intersection where at least fifty people surrounded a huge brass counter.

Although he had intended to order a rum, he said mechanically, because of what he had drunk at the Grelot:

'A marc.'

Lulu had hung around here just as others were hanging around at this moment, attentive to the glances of the men.

He headed for the phone booth, slipped a token in the machine and dialled the number of Quai des Orfèvres. He didn't know who was on duty. He recognized the voice of a newcomer named Lucien, who had been a good student and was already preparing for his exams in order to rise in rank.

'Maigret here. Anything new?'

'No, sir. Except for two Arabs who got into a knife fight in Rue de la Goutte d'Or. One of them died as they were putting him on the stretcher. The other was wounded but managed to get away.'

It was no more than 300 metres from where he was now. It had happened barely twenty minutes earlier, probably as he was walking along Boulevard de La Chapelle. He had known nothing, heard nothing. The killer might have passed him. Other dramas would occur in the neighbourhood before the night was over, probably one or two that would come to light immediately, others the police would only hear about much later.

Pierrot, too, had gone to ground between Barbès and La Villette.

Had he known that Lulu was pregnant? Was it to tell him the news that she had phoned him at the Grelot to come and see her?

Dr Paul had said six weeks. That meant she must have suspected it for a few days.

Had she told Étienne Gouin?

It was possible, but not likely. She was more the kind of girl who would go to see a local doctor or a midwife.

He could only speculate. Once back home, she hadn't come to a decision for a while. According to Madame Gouin, the professor had gone to see Lulu after his dinner but had only stayed for a few minutes.

Back at the bar, Maigret ordered another drink. He had no desire to leave immediately. It struck him that this was an ideal place to think about Lulu and Pierrot.

'She didn't tell Gouin,' he muttered under his breath.

It was in Pierre Eyraud she must have confided at first, which explained his hurried visit.

In that case, could he have killed her?

First, it was necessary to be sure she knew about her condition. If she had lived in another neighbourhood, he would have been convinced she had seen a local doctor. In the Étoile, where she was always a stranger, that was less likely.

The next day, a note would have to be sent to all the doctors and midwives in Paris. That struck him as essential. Since the telephone call from Dr Paul, he had been convinced that Lulu's pregnancy was the key to the drama.

Was Gouin sleeping peacefully? Was he taking advantage of an evening off to work on some book about surgery?

It was too late to go and see the cleaning lady, Madame Brault, although she lived not far from here, near Place Clichy. Why hadn't she mentioned the professor? Was it credible that, spending every morning in the apartment as she did, she was unaware of the identity of Lulu's lover?

The two women chatted. She was the only person in the building who could have understood what someone like Louise Filon told her.

The concierge had kept silent at first because she had a debt of gratitude to the professor and might well have been more or less consciously in love with him.

It was as if all these women were determined to protect him. The prestige this sixty-two-year-old man enjoyed among them was not the least curious aspect of this case.

He did nothing to win them over. He used them almost distractedly, in order to obtain a physical release, yet none of them seemed to resent this cynical attitude of his.

Maigret would have to question his assistant, Lucile Decaux. And also, perhaps, Madame Gouin's sister, the only woman so far over whom the professor seemed to have no hold.

'How much do I owe you?'

He got in the first taxi he found.

'Boulevard Richard-Lenoir.'

'I know, Monsieur Maigret.'

That gave him the idea that they should look for the taxi that had brought Gouin home from the hospital the previous evening.

He felt heavy, numbed by the marc he had drunk, and he half closed his eyes as the lights glided past on either side of the car.

It was Lulu he kept coming back to. He took his wallet from his pocket and looked at her photographs in the half-light of the taxi. Her mother hadn't smiled either when she had had her photograph taken.

5.

The following morning, he had an unpleasant taste of marc in his mouth and when, at about 9.15, during the daily briefing, he was told that he was wanted on the telephone, he had the impression that his breath still stank of cheap alcohol and he avoided speaking too closely to his colleagues.

All the heads of department were present in the commissioner's office overlooking the Seine, as they were every morning, all of them holding files of varying thickness. It was still grey, the river was a nasty colour, and people were walking as quickly as the day before, especially those crossing the windswept Pont Saint-Michel, the men raising their arms to hold on to their hats, the women lowering theirs to keep their skirts in place.

'You can take the call here.'

'I'm afraid it might be a long one, chief. It's best if I go to my office.'

The others, who couldn't all have drunk marc the previous evening, didn't look any better than he did, and everyone seemed in a bad mood. It must have been an effect of the light.

'Is that you, chief?'

Maigret sensed a certain excitement in Janvier's voice.

'What's happened?'

'He just dropped in. Do you want me to tell you in detail?'

Janvier, who had slept on the sofa in Lulu's apartment, couldn't have been looking too good either.

'I'm listening.'

'Here goes. It happened a few minutes ago, no more than ten. I was in the kitchen, drinking a cup of coffee I'd made myself. I didn't have either my jacket or tie on. I have to tell you, I didn't get to sleep until quite late.'

'Was it a quiet evening?'

'I didn't hear anything. I couldn't sleep, that's all.'

'Carry on.'

'You'll see, it was all quite simple. So simple, I still can't get over it. I heard a slight noise, a key turning in the lock. I kept still, but placed myself so that I could see into the living room. Someone came into the hall, crossed it and opened the second door. It was the professor, who's taller and thinner than I'd imagined. He was wearing a long dark overcoat, with a woollen scarf around his neck, and he had his hat and gloves on.'

'What did he do?'

'That's just it. That's what I'm trying to explain. He didn't do anything. He took two or three steps forward, slowly, like a man coming home. I wondered for a moment what it was he was staring at, and then I realized it was my shoes, which I'd left on the carpet. When he turned his head, he saw me and frowned. Slightly. He didn't flinch. He didn't seem either embarrassed or frightened.

'He looked at me like someone whose mind is on something else and who needs a moment to come back down to earth. Finally, he asked without raising his voice, "Are you from the police?"

'I was so surprised by his appearance, the way he was taking things, that all I could do was nod.

'We were both silent for a while, and from the way he was staring at my bare feet, I had the impression he wasn't pleased with my lack of consideration. It's just an impression. Perhaps he wasn't bothered about my feet at all.

'I managed to say, "What are you doing here, professor?"

'"So you know who I am?"

'He's a man who gives you the feeling that you're nothing at all, that even when his eyes come to rest on you, you don't matter any more to him than a flower on the wallpaper.

'"I haven't come for any particular reason," he said. "I just wanted to have a look."

'And that's what he did, he looked at the sofa where the pillow and blanket I'd been using still were, and sniffed the smell of coffee.

'Still in a neutral voice, he said, "I'm surprised your boss hasn't been keen to question me. You can tell him, young man, that I'm at his disposal. I'm going to Cochin now and I'll be there until eleven. Then I'll drop by the Saint-Joseph clinic before going home for lunch. This afternoon, I have a major operation at the American hospital in Neuilly."

'He looked around again, then turned and went out, closing both doors behind him.

'I opened the window to watch him leave. A taxi was parked outside the building, and a young woman was waiting for him in the middle of the pavement with a black briefcase under her arm. She opened the door of the cab for him and got in behind him.

'I assume that when she comes to fetch him in the morning she phones him from the lodge to tell him she's downstairs.

'That's all, chief.'

'Thanks.'

'Do you think he's rich?'

'They say he earns a lot. He operates on poor patients for free, but, when he does work for money, he demands exorbitant fees. Why do you ask?'

'Because last night, as I couldn't sleep, I made an inventory of the girl's things. They aren't what I was expecting to find. Yes, there are two fur coats, but they aren't top quality, and one of them is sheepskin. Not a single item, from the underwear to the shoes, comes from a well-known shop. It obviously isn't what she wore in Barbès, but nor are they the kind of clothes you'd expect to find in the apartment of a woman kept by a rich man. I didn't find a chequebook, or anything to indicate that she has a bank account, but there are only a few thousand-franc notes in her handbag and two more in the drawer of the bedside table.'

'I think you can come back. Do you have a key?'

'I saw one in the handbag.'

'Lock the door when you leave. Put a thread or something on it so that we'll know if it's been opened. Has the cleaning lady been in?'

He had not told her the day before whether or not she could come back to clean the apartment. It hadn't occurred to anyone that she hadn't been paid.

There was no point going back to the commissioner's office, where the daily briefing would be over by now. Lober was still in Rue Briquet, most likely tired and chilled to the bone, although he'd probably warmed himself with a few glasses of rum since the bistros had opened.

Maigret called the Goutte d'Or police station.

'Is Janin there? Hasn't he been in this morning? This is Maigret. Could you send someone to Rue Briquet, where they'll find one of my inspectors, Lober? They can tell him that unless there's anything new he should phone in his report and go home to bed.'

Coming back from Barbès the previous evening, he had made up his mind to do various things this morning, and now he had to make an effort to remember them. He called Lucas.

'How are things?'

'Fine, chief. There was a time last night when two cycle officers in the twentieth arrondissement thought they'd laid their hands on Pierrot. They took the man to the nearest station. It wasn't Pierrot, but a young man who looks like him and who also happens to be a musician, in a brasserie on Place Blanche.'

'I'd like you to phone Béziers. Try to find out if a man named Ernest Filon, who was in the hospital in that town several years ago, still lives in the region.'

'Got it.'

'I'd also like the taxi drivers who usually park around Cochin in the evening to be questioned. One of them must have driven the professor home the day before yesterday.'

'Anything else?'

'That's it for now.'

It was all part of the routine. And awaiting him on his desk was a whole pile of documents that needed signing, apart from the reports from the pathologist and from Gastine-Renette, which he had to transmit to the prosecutor's department.

He interrupted his work to ask for the telephone number of his friend Pardon, who was a doctor and whom he saw more or less regularly every month.

'Are you very busy?'

'Four or five patients in the waiting room. Less than usual for this time of year.'

'Do you know Professor Gouin?'

'Several of my patients have been operated on by him, and I was present at the operations.'

'What do you think of him?'

'He's one of the finest doctors, not only that we have now, but that we've ever had. Unlike many surgeons, he isn't just a hand, he's a brain. Thanks to him, there have been a number of discoveries that are really important and will remain important.'

'And as a man?'

'What exactly do you want to know?'

'What you think of him.'

'It's hard to say. He isn't very sociable, especially with an ordinary family doctor like me. But they say he's distant with other people, too.'

'So he isn't liked?'

'I'd say he's more feared. He has a way of answering the questions you dare to ask him. Apparently he's even harder with some of his patients. The story goes that an extremely rich old woman once begged him to operate on her and offered him a fortune. You know what he replied?

'"The operation would gain you two weeks, perhaps a month. The time I spent on it might save the entire life of another patient."'

'Apart from that, the staff at Cochin love him.'

'Especially the women?'

'Oh, you've heard about that? Apparently as far as that goes, he's quite something. Sometimes, immediately after an operation, he . . . You know what I mean?'

'Yes. Is that all?'

'He's still a great man despite that.'

'Thanks, old man.'

Without really knowing why, he felt like talking to Désirée Brault. He could have summoned her, or had someone fetch her. It was the way most of the other heads of department worked: some of them didn't leave their offices all day.

He dropped in on Lucas, who was busy phoning.

'I'm going out for an hour or two.'

He took one of the cars and had himself driven to Rue Nollet, behind Place Clichy, where Lulu's cleaning lady lived. The building was in a state of disrepair and clearly hadn't received a coat of paint in more than twenty years. The families crammed into it overflowed on to the landings, with children playing on the stairs.

Madame Brault lived on the fourth floor, on the courtyard side. There was no lift, and the stairs were steep. Maigret had to stop twice on the way up, sniffing more or less pleasant smells.

'Who is it?' cried a voice when he knocked at the door. 'Come in. I can't open.'

She was in the kitchen, in her slip, barefoot, doing her washing in a galvanized iron bowl. She didn't look surprised when she saw Maigret, didn't say hello, merely waited for him to speak.

'I dropped by to see you.'

'Well, well!'

Because of the washing, the windowpanes were all steamed up. There was the sound of snoring in the next room, where Maigret noticed the foot of a bed, and Madame Brault went and shut the door.

'My husband's asleep,' she said.

'Drunk?'

'Just for a change.'

'When I spoke to you yesterday, why didn't you tell me who Lulu's long-term lover was?'

'Because you didn't ask me. I remember it perfectly well. You asked me if I'd ever seen a man visiting her.'

'And you never saw him?'

'No.'

'But you knew it was the professor?'

From her manner, it was clear that she knew a lot more. Only, she wouldn't say anything, unless she was forced to. Not because she herself had anything to hide. Nor, probably, because she was protecting someone. In her case, it was a matter of principle not to help the police, which was quite natural, when it came down to it, given that they had been hounding her all her life. She didn't like policemen. They were her natural enemies.

'Did your employer talk to you about him?'

'From time to time.'

'What did she tell you about him?'

'She told me so many things!'

'Did she want to leave him?'

'I don't know if she really wanted to leave him, but she wasn't happy in the building.'

Without being asked, he had sat down on a chair, making its straw bottom creak.

'What was stopping her from leaving?'

'I didn't ask her.'

'Was she in love with Pierrot?'

'That's the impression I got.'

'Did she get a lot of money from Gouin?'

'He gave her money when she wanted it.'

'Did she want it often?'

'As soon as there was none left in the apartment. Sometimes I only found small notes in her bag and in the drawer when I was about to go shopping. I'd tell her, and she'd say, "I'll ask for some later."'

'Did she give some of it to Pierrot?'

'That's none of my business. If she'd been smarter . . .'

She broke off.

'What would have happened?'

'First of all, she would never have gone to live in that building, where she seemed like a prisoner.'

'Didn't he let her go out?'

'Most of the time, she was the one who didn't dare go out, for fear that monsieur might suddenly decide to drop by and say hello. She wasn't his mistress, she was a kind of maid, except that what he expected of her wasn't to work, but to go to bed with him. If she'd continued to have an apartment somewhere else and it was him who had to make an effort . . . But what's the point of all this? What exactly do you want of me?'

'Information.'

'Today, you come for information and you take your hat off. Tomorrow, if I'm unfortunate enough to stop at a shop counter, you'll have me thrown in jail. What information do you need?'

She was hanging up her washing on a line that crossed the kitchen.

'Did you know that Lulu was pregnant?'

She turned abruptly.

'Who told you that?'

'The post-mortem.'

'So she wasn't wrong.'

'When did she tell you?'

'Maybe three days before someone put a bullet in her head.'

'Wasn't she sure?'

'No. She hadn't yet been to the doctor. She was afraid of going.'

'Why?'

'For fear of being disappointed, I suppose.'

'She wanted a child?'

'I think she was pleased to be pregnant. It was still too early to celebrate. I told her that these days doctors have a thing that can tell you for sure, even after two or three weeks.'

'Did she go to see a doctor?'

'She asked me if I knew one, and I gave her the address of someone I know near here, in Rue des Dames.'

'Do you know if she saw him?'

'If she did, she didn't tell me.'

'Did Pierrot know?'

'Do you know anything about women? Have you ever met a woman who talks about these things to a man before she's sure?'

'So you don't think she told the professor either?'

'Try to use your common sense.'

'What do you think would have happened if she hadn't been killed?'

'I can't read tea leaves.'

'Would she have kept the child?'

'Definitely.'

'Would she have stayed with the professor?'

'Unless she'd left with Pierrot.'

'Who do you think was the father?'

This time, too, she looked at him as if he knew nothing about anything.

'You don't imagine it was the old man?'

'It happens.'

'You read about it in the newspapers. Only, as women aren't cows who are kept in a shed and led to the bull once a year, it's hard to swear on anything.'

In the next room, her husband was moving on the bed and groaning. She went and opened the door.

'Hold on, Jules, I'm with someone! I'll bring you your drink in a few minutes.'

And turning to Maigret:

'Do you have any more questions?'

'Not exactly. Did you hate Professor Gouin?'

'I told you, I never saw him.'

'But you hated him anyway?'

'I hate all those people.'

'Supposing when you got there in the morning you saw a gun in Lulu's hand, or on the carpet, within easy reach of that hand. Wouldn't you have been tempted to get rid of it, so as to rule out suicide and get the professor into trouble?'

'Don't you ever get tired? Do you think I'm so stupid that I don't know that, when the police have the choice between a big shot and a poor devil of a musician like Pierrot, it's the poor devil they'll go after?'

She poured some coffee into a bowl, sugared it and called to her husband:

'I'm coming!'

Maigret didn't insist. It was only when he was at the door that he turned and asked her for the name and address of the doctor in Rue des Dames.

The doctor's name was Duclos. He hadn't been practising there for long. In fact, he had probably only just qualified, because his consulting room was almost bare, with merely the essential instruments, all second-hand. When Maigret told him who he was, he seemed to understand immediately.

'I knew somebody would come and see me sooner or later.'

'Did she give you her name?'

'Yes. I even filled out her record.'

'How long had she known she was pregnant?'

The doctor seemed more like a student and, to make himself look important, consulted his almost empty patient files.

'She came on Saturday. She was sent by a woman I treated.'

'Madame Brault, I know.'

'She told me she might be pregnant and she needed to be sure.'

'Hold on a moment. Did she seem worried?'

'I can only reply no. When a girl like her asks me that question, I expect her to ask me if I'll do what I have to do to give her an abortion. That happens twenty times a week. I don't know if it's the same in other neighbourhoods. Anyway, I gave her a thorough examination. I asked her for the usual urine sample. She wanted to know what happened then, and I explained about the rabbit test.'

'What was her reaction?'

'She wanted to know if we had to kill the rabbit. I told her to come back on Monday afternoon.'

'Did she come?'

'Yes, at half past five. I told her she was well and truly pregnant, and she thanked me.'

'Did she say anything else?'

'She asked me if I was absolutely sure, and I said I was.'

'Did she seem happy?'

'I'd swear she did.'

So at about six o'clock on Monday Lulu had left Rue des Dames and gone back to Avenue Carnot. At about eight, having finished dinner, the professor, according to Madame Gouin, spent a few minutes in the apartment on the fourth floor, then went to the hospital.

Up until about ten o'clock, Louise Filon had been alone at home. She had eaten tinned lobster and drunk a little wine. Apparently she had then gone to bed, since the bed had been found unmade; not untidy, as if she had slept with a man, but simply unmade.

By then, Pierrot was already at the Grelot, and she could have telephoned him immediately. But she hadn't called him until about 9.30.

Was it to tell him the news that she had made him come all the way to the Étoile during his work hours? If so, why had she waited so long?

Pierrot had jumped in a taxi. According to the concierge, he had stayed in the apartment for about twenty minutes.

Gouin, according to both the concierge and his wife, had come back from the hospital just after eleven and hadn't dropped in on his mistress.

The following morning, at eight o'clock, Madame Brault, arriving to do her work, had found Louise dead on the sofa in the living room. She claimed there was no weapon near the body.

Dr Paul, always cautious in his conclusions, placed the time of death between nine and eleven. Because of the phone call to the Grelot, you could substitute 9.30 for nine.

As for the fingerprints found in the apartment, they belonged to only four people: Lulu herself, the cleaning lady, the professor and Pierre Eyraud. Moers had sent someone to Cochin to photograph Gouin's prints on a form he had just signed at the hospital. For the three others, they hadn't had to go to any trouble, given that they all had criminal records.

Lulu had obviously not expected to be attacked, since she had been shot at close range.

The apartment had not been ransacked, which indicated that the killer had not killed for money, or to get hold of some document or other.

'Many thanks, doctor. I assume that after her visit nobody came to question you about her? And nobody phoned you to talk to you about her?'

'No. When I read in the newspaper that she'd been killed, I expected a visit from the police, given that it was her cleaning lady who sent her to me and she must have known. To tell the truth, if you hadn't come this morning, I had the intention, just in case, of phoning you in the afternoon.'

Soon afterwards, Maigret telephoned Madame Gouin from a bistro in Rue des Dames. She recognized his voice and didn't seem surprised.

'I'm listening.'

'You told me yesterday that your sister works in a library. May I ask you which one?'

'The municipal library on Place Saint-Sulpice.'

'Many thanks.'

'Have you found out anything?'

'Only that Louise Filon was pregnant.'

'Oh!'

He was sorry he had mentioned it over the phone, unable as he was to judge her reaction.

'Does that surprise you?'

'Yes, it does, rather . . . It's probably ridiculous, but you never expect that of certain women. You forget they're built just like the rest of us.'

'Do you know if your husband was aware of the fact?'

'He would have told me.'

'Has he ever had children?'

'No, never.'

'Didn't he want them?'

'I don't think he cared one way or the other. The fact is, we haven't had any. Probably my doing.'

The little black car took him to Place Saint-Sulpice, which, for no clear reason, was the Paris square he hated the most. Whenever he was there, he had the impression of being somewhere in the provinces. Even the shops struck him as looking different, and the passers-by seemed slower and drabber.

The library was particularly drab, dimly lit and as silent as an empty church. At this hour, there were only three or four people, regulars probably, looking through the dusty books.

Antoinette Ollivier, Madame Gouin's sister, watched him advance towards her. She looked older than her fifty years and had the somewhat contemptuous self-confidence of those women who think they know the truth about everything.

'Detective Chief Inspector Maigret of the Police Judiciaire.'

'I recognized you from your photographs.'

As in church, she spoke in a low voice, although he was reminded more of a school than a church when she invited him to sit down at the green baize table that served as her desk. She was fatter than her sister Germaine, but it was a kind of fat that seemed barely alive, and her skin was a neutral colour like that of some nuns.

'I assume you're here to ask me some questions?'

'You assume correctly. Your sister told me you paid her a visit yesterday evening.'

'That's right. I arrived at about half past eight and left at half past eleven, immediately after *that man* came home.'

She must have thought it the height of contempt to not even utter her brother-in-law's name, and she seemed quite pleased with the words *that man*, detaching the syllables.

'Do you often spend the evening with your sister?'

For some reason, it struck Maigret that she was on her guard and that she would be even more reticent than the concierge or Madame Brault.

The others responded cautiously because they were afraid of harming the professor.

This woman, on the contrary, was probably afraid of exonerating him.

'No, not often,' she replied reluctantly.

'Meaning once every six months, once a year, once every two years?'

'Perhaps once a year.'

'Did you fix an appointment?'

'You don't fix an appointment with your sister.'

'So you went there without knowing if she was going to be in? Do you have a telephone in your apartment?'

'Yes.'

'But you didn't call your sister?'

'She called me.'

'To ask you to come over?'

'It wasn't as specific as that. She talked about various things.'

'What kind of things?'

'Family things, mainly. She doesn't write much. I'm more in contact with our other brothers and sisters than she is.'

'Did she say she'd like to see you?'

'More or less. She asked me if I was free.'

'What time was that?'

'About half past six. I'd just got home and was making dinner.'

'Were you surprised?'

'No. I simply made sure he wouldn't be there. What has he told you?'

'You mean Professor Gouin?'

'Yes.'

'I haven't questioned him yet.'

'Is that because you assume he's innocent? Because he's a famous surgeon, a member of the Academy of Medicine and—'

Although she hadn't raised her voice, it had become more resonant with emotion now.

'What happened when you got to Avenue Carnot?' he cut in.

'I went upstairs, kissed my sister on the cheek and took off my hat and coat.'

'Where did you go?'

'To the little room next to Germaine's bedroom, the one she calls her boudoir. There's something sinister about the big drawing room, and it's almost never used.'

'What did you do?'

'What two sisters our age do when they see each other after several months. We chatted. I gave her the news about everybody. In particular, I told her about François, a nephew of ours who was ordained a priest a year ago and is about to leave for Northern Canada as a missionary.'

'Did you have anything to drink?'

The question surprised her, shocked her to the point that her cheeks turned red. 'We had a cup of coffee to start with.'

'And then?'

'I sneezed several times. I told my sister I was afraid I might have caught a head cold coming out of the Métro, where the heat was stifling. It was too hot at my sister's, too.'

'Were the servants in the apartment?'

'They both went upstairs at about nine, after coming to say goodnight. My sister has had the same cook for twelve years. The maids change more often, for an obvious reason.'

He didn't ask the reason; he had understood.

'So, you sneezed . . .'

'Germaine suggested a couple of toddies and went to the kitchen to make them.'

'What did you do during that time?'

'I read a magazine article in which there was a mention of our village.'

'Was your sister absent for a long time?'

'Long enough to boil two glasses of water.'

'The other times you were there, did you wait for your brother-in-law to get home before you left?'

'I avoid meeting him as much as possible.'

'Were you surprised when you saw him come in?'

'My sister had assured me he wouldn't be back before midnight.'

'How did he seem?'

'The way he always does, like a man who thinks he's above the rules of morality and decency.'

'You didn't notice anything special about him?'

'I didn't bother to look at him. I put on my hat and coat and slammed the door on my way out.'

'During the evening, did you hear any noise that might have been a gunshot?'

'No. Until about eleven, someone was playing the piano in the building, on the floor above. I recognized Chopin.'

'Did you know your brother-in-law's mistress was pregnant?'

'That doesn't surprise me.'

'Did your sister tell you?'

'She didn't talk to me about the girl.'

'Did she *ever* talk to you about her?'

'No.'

'But you knew about her?'

She blushed again. 'She must have mentioned her at the beginning, when *that man* set her up in the building.'

'Did it bother her?'

'We all think in different ways. And you don't live for years with a man like that without it rubbing off on you in the end.'

'In other words, your sister didn't blame her husband for the affair and wasn't upset by Louise Filon's presence in the building?'

'What are you getting at?'

He would have been hard put to answer that question. He had the feeling that he was digging further and further without knowing where he would end up, anxious to get a more precise idea of the people who had been in contact with Lulu, and of Lulu herself.

A young man who wanted some books disturbed them, and Antoinette left Maigret for five or six minutes. When she returned, she had drawn on even deeper reserves of hatred for her brother-in-law and didn't give Maigret time to open his mouth.

'When are you going to arrest him?'

'Do you think he killed Louise Filon?'

'Who else could it have been?'

'Her boyfriend Pierrot, for instance.'

'Why would he have done that?'

'Out of jealousy, or because she was planning to break up with him.'

'What about *that man*? Do you imagine *he* wasn't jealous? Do you think a man his age doesn't get upset over a girl choosing a young man over him? What if *he* was the one she'd decided to break up with?'

She seemed to be trying to hypnotize him, the better to get the idea of the professor's guilt into his head.

'If you knew him better, you'd realize he isn't the kind of man who'd think twice about getting rid of a human being.'

'On the contrary, I thought he was devoted to saving lives.'

'That's vanity! To show the world that he's the greatest surgeon of our time. The proof of that is that he only accepts difficult operations.'

'Perhaps because others can take care of the easier ones.'

'You're defending him without knowing him.'

'I'm trying to understand.'

'It's not as complicated as all that.'

'You forget that, according to the pathologist, who's rarely wrong, the murder was committed before eleven o'clock. It was after eleven when the concierge saw the professor come home, and he went straight up to the fourth floor.'

'What's there to prove he didn't come back earlier?'

'I assume it's easy enough to check his timetable with the hospital.'

'Have you done so?'

It was Maigret's turn to almost blush.

'Not yet.'

'Well, do it, then! It'll probably be more worthwhile than hunting a young man who hasn't done anything.'

'Do you hate the professor?'

'Him and all those like him.'

She said this with such force that the three people in the library raised their heads from their books at the same time.

'You're forgetting your hat!'

'I thought I'd left it in the entrance.'

With a scornful finger, she pointed to it on the green baize of the table, where the presence of a man's hat probably constituted unseemly behaviour in her eyes.

6.

Technically, as it were, Antoinette wasn't so wrong.

By the time Maigret got to the Cochin hospital on Faubourg Saint-Jacques, Étienne Gouin had already left for the Saint-Joseph Clinic in Passy, together with his assistant. Maigret had expected that, since it was after eleven. But he wasn't here to see the professor. Perhaps, when it came down to it, he didn't want to meet him face to face just yet, although he didn't quite know why.

Gouin's department was on the second floor, and Maigret had to negotiate with the office staff before he was given permission to go upstairs. He found the long corridor more animated than he had expected, the nurses under great pressure. The one he approached as she came out of one of the rooms, looking less busy than the others, was a middle-aged woman with already white hair.

'Are you the head nurse?'

'The head nurse for the day shift.'

He told her who he was, and that he would like to ask her a few questions.

'What about?'

He hesitated to admit that it was about the professor. She had led him to the door of a small office but didn't invite him in.

'Is that the operating theatre I can see at the end of the corridor?'

'One of the operating theatres, yes.'

'What happens when a surgeon spends part of the night in the hospital?'

'I don't understand. You mean when a surgeon comes here to perform an operation?'

'No. Unless I'm mistaken, they're sometimes here for other reasons – if they're afraid there might be complications, for example, or else to wait for the result of their operation.'

'That does happen. What of it?'

'Where do they go?'

'That depends.'

'On what?'

'On how long they stay. If they aren't here for long, they come to my office, or walk up and down the corridor. But if they have to wait for several hours, in case an emergency operation is necessary, they go upstairs, to the interns' section, where there are two or three rooms at their disposal.'

'Do they use the stairs?'

'Either that or the lift. The rooms are on the fourth floor. Most of the time, they rest until they're called.'

She was clearly wondering what these questions were in aid of. The newspapers hadn't mentioned Gouin's name in connection with the death of Lulu. It was likely that nobody here knew of his relations with the girlfriend of Pierrot the Musician.

'I don't suppose I can speak to someone who was here the night before last?'

'After eight o'clock?'

'Yes. I should have said the night of Monday to Tuesday.'

'The nurses who are here now are all like me. They belong to the day team. It may be that one of the interns was on duty. Wait a moment.'

She went into two or three rooms and at last came back with a tall, bony, red-haired young man wearing thick spectacles.

'Someone from the police,' she said and went and sat down in her office, but didn't ask them in.

Maigret introduced himself.

'Detective Chief Inspector Maigret.'

'I thought I recognized you. What would you like to know?'

'Were you here on the night of Monday to Tuesday?'

'Most of the night, yes. The professor operated on a child on Monday afternoon. It was a difficult case, and he asked me to keep a close eye on the patient.'

'Didn't he come himself?'

'He spent most of the evening in the hospital.'

'Was he on this floor with you?'

'He got here just after eight, with his assistant. We went in together to see the patient and stayed there, looking out for something that didn't in fact happen. I don't suppose you want me to go into technical details?'

'I probably wouldn't understand a thing. So you stayed with the patient for an hour or two?'

'Less than an hour. Mademoiselle Decaux insisted on the professor getting some rest, because he'd performed an emergency operation the previous night. In the end, he went upstairs to have a lie down.'

'How was he dressed?'

'He wasn't expecting to operate. And in fact he didn't have to. He was still in his normal everyday clothes.'

'Did Mademoiselle Decaux keep you company?'

'Yes. We chatted. The professor came down just before eleven. I'd been in to see the patient every quarter of an hour. We went back together and, as the patient seemed out of danger, the professor decided to go home.'

'Did he leave with Mademoiselle Decaux?'

'They almost always arrive and leave together.'

'So, from a quarter to nine to eleven o'clock, Gouin was alone on the fourth floor.'

'Alone in a room, in any case. I still don't see why you're asking these questions.'

'Could he have come down without your seeing him?'

'By the stairs, yes.'

'Could he also have passed the desk downstairs without anybody noticing?'

'Possibly. Nobody pays any attention to doctors going in and out, especially at night.'

'I'm very grateful. Do you mind telling me your name?'

'Mansuy. Raoul Mansuy.'

This was where Madame Gouin's sister hadn't been so wrong. Physically speaking, Étienne Gouin could have left the hospital and had himself driven to Avenue Carnot and back without anyone noticing his absence.

'I don't suppose I'm allowed to know why . . .' the intern began just as Maigret was about to walk away.

Maigret shook his head. He went downstairs and crossed the courtyard to the little black car and the police driver waiting at the kerb. When he got to Quai des Orfèvres, he didn't think of casting his usual glance through the windows of the waiting room. Before entering his office, he passed through the inspectors' room, where Lucas stood up to talk to him.

'I have some information from Béziers.'

Maigret had almost forgotten about Louise Filon's father.

'The man died of cirrhosis of the liver three years ago. Before that, he worked on and off in the town abattoir.'

Nobody had yet come forward to claim Louise's inheritance, if there was one.

'Someone named Louis has been waiting for you next door for the last half-hour.'

'A musician.'

'I think so.'

'Bring him to my office.'

Maigret went in, took off his hat and coat, sat down in his place and picked up one of the pipes arranged in front of the desk blotter. A few moments later, the accordion player was admitted, looking uneasy, peering about him before sitting down as if expecting a trap.

'You can leave us, Lucas.'

And, to Louis:

'If you're going to be here for a while, I advise you to take your coat off.'

'There's no need. He phoned me.'

'When?'

'This morning, just after nine.'

He was observing Maigret hesitantly.

'Are we still on?'

'Are you referring to what I said yesterday? Of course. If Pierrot's innocent, he has nothing to fear.'

'He didn't kill her. He would have told me. I did what you asked, I told him you were ready to meet him where he wanted and that then he'd be free again.'

'Let's be clear about this. I don't want there to be any misunderstanding. If I think he's innocent, he'll be entirely free. If I think he's guilty, or if I have any doubts, I guarantee I won't take advantage of our encounter, in other words, I'll let him go, but then the search will resume.'

'That's pretty much what I told him.'

'And what did he say?'

'That he was ready to see you. He has nothing to hide.'

'Would he come here?'

'Provided he isn't besieged by reporters and photographers. Provided also he can get here without the cops jumping him.'

Louis was speaking slowly, weighing his words, without taking his eyes off Maigret.

'Could it be done soon?' Maigret asked.

He checked the time. It wasn't yet midday. Between midday and two o'clock, the offices of Quai des Orfèvres were quiet and almost deserted. It was the time of day Maigret chose as often as possible when he had to set up a difficult interrogation.

'He could be here in half an hour.'

'In that case, listen to me. I assume he has pocket money. Let him take a taxi and ask to be dropped outside the prison on Quai de l'Horloge. Not many people pass that way. Nobody will pay any attention to him. One of my inspectors will wait for him at the door and bring him to me through the interior of the Palais de Justice.'

Getting to his feet, Louis looked at Maigret again for a moment or two, conscious of the responsibility he was assuming on behalf of his friend.

'I believe you,' he sighed at last. 'Half an hour, an hour tops.'

When he had left, Maigret phoned the Brasserie Dauphine to ask for some food to be brought up.

'Enough for two people. And four glasses of beer.'

Then he called his wife and told her he wouldn't be home for lunch.

Finally, just to be sure, he went upstairs to the commissioner's office, preferring to inform him about the experiment he was going to attempt.

'Do you think he's innocent?'

'Until proven otherwise. If he was guilty, he'd have no reason to come and see me. Or else he's tougher than I thought.'

'What about the professor?'

'I don't know. I still have no idea.'

'Have you talked to him?'

'No. Janvier had a brief conversation with him.'

The commissioner sensed it was useless to ask questions. Maigret had that heavy, stubborn air about him that everyone at headquarters knew so well. At such times, he was even less talkative than usual.

'The girl was pregnant,' he simply added, as if it was bothering him.

He went back to the inspectors' room. Lucas had not yet gone to lunch.

'I don't suppose the taxi's been found?'

'There's no chance we'll find it before tonight. The drivers who work nights are all in bed.'

'It might not be a bad idea to look for two taxis.'

'I don't understand.'

'It's quite possible that earlier in the evening, just before ten, the professor had himself driven to Avenue Carnot and then back to the hospital.'

'I'll have it checked.'

He looked round for the inspector he would send to wait outside the prison and take charge of Pierrot and chose young Lapointe.

'Go and stand on the pavement opposite the prison. After a while, you'll see someone get out of a taxi. It'll be the saxophone player.'

'Is he giving himself up?'

'He's coming to talk to me. Be nice to him. Try not to scare him. Bring him to me by way of the little courtyard and the corridors of the Palais de Justice. I promised him he wouldn't encounter any reporters.'

There were almost always some prowling in the corridors, but it was easy to get rid of them for a moment.

By the time Maigret got back to his office, the beer and sandwiches were waiting for him on a tray. He drank one of the beers but didn't start to eat and then spent a quarter of an hour standing by the window watching the barges glide by on the grey water.

At last he heard the footsteps of two men. He opened the door and signalled to Lapointe that he could go.

'Come in, Pierrot.'

The musician, pale, with bags under his eyes, was visibly upset. Just as his friend had done, he began by looking around him like a man expecting a trap.

'There's only you and me in the room,' Maigret reassured him. 'You can take your coat off. Give it to me.'

He placed it on the back of a chair.

'Are you thirsty?'

He handed him a glass of beer and took one for himself.

'Sit down. I suspected you'd come.'

'Why?'

His voice was hoarse, the voice of someone who hasn't slept all night and has smoked one cigarette after another. Two fingers of his right hand had brown tobacco stains on them. He was unshaven. Wherever it was he had gone to earth, he probably hadn't had the chance to shave.

'Have you eaten?'

'I'm not hungry.'

He seemed younger than his age and he was so nervous, it was tiring to look at him. Even seated, he was still trembling from head to foot.

'You promised . . .' he began.

'I'll keep my word.'

'I came of my own free will.'

'You did the right thing.'

'I didn't kill Lulu.'

Suddenly, when Maigret was least expecting it, he burst into tears. It was clearly the first time he had let himself go since he had learned of his girlfriend's death. He wept like a child, hiding his face with both hands, and Maigret was careful not to interrupt him. Basically, ever since he had found out from the newspaper in the little restaurant on Boulevard Barbès that Lulu was dead, he hadn't had time to think about her, but only about the threat hanging over him.

Overnight, he had become a hunted man, his freedom – if not his head – at stake with every passing minute.

Now that he was at Quai des Orfèvres, face to face with the police, who had been his nightmare, he was suddenly letting himself go.

'I swear I didn't kill her,' he repeated.

Maigret believed him. He didn't look or sound like a guilty man. Louis had been right, the previous day, when he had talked about his friend as a weak man who acted tough.

With his fair hair, his bright eyes, his almost chubby face, it wasn't a butcher's boy he made you think of, but an office clerk. You could imagine him strolling on the Champs-Élysées with his wife on a Sunday afternoon.

'Did you really believe it was me?'

'No.'

'So why did you tell that to the papers?'

'I never said a word to the reporters. They write what they want. And the circumstances—'

'I didn't kill her.'

'Calm down now. You can smoke.'

Pierrot's hand was still shaking as he lit his cigarette.

'There's one question I have to ask you before anything else. When you went to Avenue Carnot on Monday night, was Louise still alive?'

Pierrot opened his eyes wide.

'Of course!' he exclaimed.

It was probably the truth, otherwise he wouldn't have waited to read the paper at midday the following day to take fright and run away.

'When she phoned you at the Grelot, did you have any idea what she had to say to you?'

'No, I had no idea. She was in a nervous state and wanted to talk to me right away.'

'What did you think?'

'That she'd made up her mind.'

'To do what?'

'To give it all up.'

'Give up what exactly?'

'The old man.'

'Had you asked her to?'

'I'd been begging her to come and live with me for the past two years.'

He added, as if challenging Maigret, as if challenging the whole world:

'I love her!'

He wasn't being assertive. On the contrary, he spoke haltingly.

'Are you sure you don't want a bite to eat?'

This time, Pierrot automatically grabbed a sandwich, and Maigret took another. It was better this way. Both were eating, and that relaxed the atmosphere. No noise could be heard from the offices, except the tapping of a type-writer somewhere.

'Had Lulu ever before called you to Avenue Carnot when you were at work?'

'No. Not to Avenue Carnot. Once, when she was still living in Rue La Fayette and she suddenly felt ill . . . It was only a bad case of indigestion, but she was afraid . . . She was always afraid of dying . . .'

Because of that word, and the images it evoked, his eyes grew wet again, and he paused for a while before biting into his sandwich.

'What did she say to you on Monday night? Hold on, though. Before you answer my question, tell me if you have a key to the apartment.'

'No.'

'Why not?'

'I don't know. No reason. I didn't go there often, and when I did she was always there to open the door.'

'So, you rang the bell and she opened the door.'

'I didn't have to ring the bell. She was listening out for me and she opened the door as soon as I got out of the lift.'

'I thought she was in bed.'

'She had been. She must have been in bed when she phoned me. She got up just before I arrived. She was in her dressing gown.'

'Did she seem normal?'

'No.'

'What kind of state was she in?'

'Hard to say. She looked as if she'd been doing a lot of thinking and was about to make a decision. I got scared when I saw her.'

'Scared of what?'

The musician hesitated.

'You might as well know,' he grunted in the end. 'I was scared because of the old man.'

'I assume you mean the professor?'

'Yes. I kept expecting him to decide to get a divorce and marry Lulu.'

'Was it on the cards?'

'If it was, she never told me.'

'Did she want him to marry her?'

'I don't know. I don't think so.'

'Did she love you?'

'I think she did.'

'Aren't you sure?'

'I don't suppose women are like men.'

'What do you mean?'

He did not clarify his thought, perhaps because he was unable to, and merely shrugged his shoulders.

'She was a poor girl,' he finally murmured as if to himself.

The mouthfuls went down his throat with difficulty, but he continued mechanically to eat.

'Where did she sit when you arrived?'

'She didn't sit down. She was too nervous to sit. She started walking up and down and said without looking at me, "I have important news to tell you." Then, as if she couldn't hold it in any longer: "I'm pregnant."'

'Did she seem pleased?'

'She didn't seem either pleased or upset.'

'Did you think the child was yours?'

He did not dare answer but, from his attitude, it was clear that for him it was obvious.

'What did you say?'

'Nothing. It had a strange effect on me. I wanted to take her in my arms.'

'Wouldn't she let you?'

'No. She kept walking up and down, talking to herself, saying things like: "I wonder what I'm going to do. This changes everything. It may be very important. If I tell him . . ."'

'She meant the professor?'

'Yes. She didn't know if she should tell him the truth or not. She wasn't sure how he'd react.'

And now Pierrot, who had finished his sandwich, sighed despondently.

'It's hard to explain. I remember the smallest details, and at the same time it's vague. I never imagined it would happen like that.'

'What had you hoped?'

'That she'd throw herself in my arms and tell me she'd finally made up her mind to come with me.'

'Had the idea occurred to her?'

'Maybe it had. I'm almost sure it had. She wanted it. In the beginning, when she came out of hospital, she claimed that she was obliged, out of gratitude, to act as she did.'

'She felt indebted to Gouin?'

'He saved her life. I think he spent more time treating her than any other of his patients.'

'Did you believe it?'

'Believe what?'

'Did you believe in Lulu's gratitude?'

'I told her she wasn't obliged to keep being his mistress. He had plenty of others.'

'Do you think he was in love with her?'

'He was definitely attached to her. I guess she'd got under his skin.'

'What about you?'

'I loved her.'

'When all's said and done, why did she send for you?'

'I've wondered that too.'

'It was about half past five that she found out for sure, at a doctor's in Rue des Dames, that she was pregnant. Couldn't she have seen you then?'

'Yes. She knew where I usually have dinner before going to the Grelot.'

'She went back home. Later, between half past seven and eight, the professor dropped in on her.'

'She told me.'

'Did she also tell you if she'd announced the news to him?'

'She hadn't told him anything.'

'She ate something and went to bed. It's likely she didn't sleep. And about nine o'clock she phoned you.'

'I know. I've thought about all that and tried to understand. But I still don't. The only thing I know for sure is that I didn't kill her.'

'Answer this question frankly, Pierrot. If on Monday evening she'd told you she didn't want to see you again, would you have killed her?'

The young man looked at him, and a vague smile rose to his lips. 'Do you want me to put a noose around my own neck?'

'You aren't obliged to answer.'

'I might have killed her. But first of all, she didn't tell me that. Secondly, I didn't have a gun.'

'You had one the last time you were arrested.'

'That was years ago, and the police didn't give it back to me. I haven't had one since. I was going to add that I wouldn't have killed her that way.'

'How would you have gone about it?'

'I don't know. I might have hit her without realizing what I was doing, or put my hands round her throat.'

He stared at the wooden floor at his feet and paused before adding in a less distinct voice:

'But maybe I wouldn't have done anything. There are things like that that you think about when you're falling asleep but that you never actually do.'

'Did you ever think about killing Lulu as you were falling asleep?'

'Yes.'

'Because you were jealous of Gouin?'

He shrugged again, which presumably meant that that wasn't the whole story, that the truth was more complicated than that.

'Before Gouin, you were already Louise Filon's boyfriend, and, unless I'm mistaken, you didn't stop her from being on the game.'

'That's different.'

Maigret was making an effort to get as close to the truth as possible, but he realized that absolute truth was elusive.

'You never took advantage of the professor's money?'

'Never!' he retorted, so sharply, with an abrupt movement of the head, that he seemed on the verge of losing his temper.

'Did Louise ever give you presents?'

'Nothing but trifles, a ring, ties, socks.'

'And you accepted them?'

'I didn't want to hurt her feelings.'

'What would you have done if she'd left Gouin?'

'We'd have lived together.'

'Like before?'

'No.'

'Why?'

'Because I never liked that.'

'What would you have lived on?'

'First of all, I earn a living.'

'Not much of one, from what Louis told me.'

'Not much of one, maybe. But I wasn't planning to stay in Paris.'

'Where did you plan to go?'

'Anywhere. South America, Canada.'

He was even younger in character than Maigret had thought.

'Lulu wasn't keen on the plan?'

'Sometimes she was tempted, and occasionally she even promised that we'd leave in a month or two.'

'I assume it was in the evening that she spoke like that?'

'How do you know?'

'And in the morning she saw things in a clearer light?'

'She was afraid.'

'Of what?'

'Of starving to death.'

They were finally getting there. There was a resentment in Pierrot that showed through in spite of him.

'Do you think it was because of that fear that she stayed with the professor?'

'Maybe.'

'She was often hungry in her life, wasn't she?'

'Just like me!' the young man retorted defiantly.

'Only, she was afraid of being hungry again.'

'What are you trying to prove?'

'Nothing yet. I'm just trying to understand. The one thing we know for sure is that on Monday night someone shot Lulu at close range. You say it wasn't you, and I believe you.'

'Are you certain you believe me?' Pierrot murmured mistrustfully.

'Until proved otherwise.'

'And you'll let me go?'

'As soon as we've finished this conversation.'

'You'll call off your search, order your men to leave me alone?'

'I'll even allow you to go back to your job at the Grelot.'

'And the newspapers?'

'I'll issue a press release in a while saying that you came to the Police Judiciaire of your own free will and that after you'd explained yourself you were allowed to go free.'

'That doesn't mean I'm not still under suspicion.'

'I'll add that there's nothing pointing to you.'

'That's something at least.'

'Did Lulu own a gun?'

'No.'

'You said just now that she was afraid.'

'Of life, of poverty, but not of people. She wouldn't have needed a gun.'

'You stayed just over a quarter of an hour at her place on Monday night?'

'I had to get back to the Grelot. Plus, I didn't like being there when the old man could come in at any minute. He has a key.'

'Did he ever do that?'

'Once.'

'What happened?'

'Nothing. It was an afternoon, at a time when he never came to see Lulu. We'd arranged to meet in town at five, but something happened that stopped me going. As I was in the area, I went up to see her. We were in the living room, chatting, when we heard the key turn in the lock. He came in. I didn't hide. He didn't look at me. He advanced into the middle of the room with his hat on his head and waited without saying a word. It was a bit as if I wasn't a human being.'

'When all's said and done, you still don't know exactly why Lulu sent for you on Monday night?'

'I assume she needed to talk to someone.'

'How did your conversation end?'

'She said, "I wanted you to know. I have no idea what I'm going to do. In any case, nothing's visible yet. You think it over, too."'

'Did Lulu ever talk to you about marrying the professor?'

He seemed to search in his memory.

'Once, when we were in a restaurant on Boulevard Rochechouart and we were talking about a girl we both knew who had just got married, she said, "If it was only up to me, he'd get a divorce and marry me."'

'Did you believe that?'

'He might have done it. At that age, men are capable of anything.'

Maigret was unable to hold back a smile. 'I won't ask you where you've been hiding since yesterday afternoon.'

'I wouldn't tell you. Am I free to go?'

'Completely.'

'And your men won't arrest me when I leave?'

'To be honest, you'd do well to spend an hour or two in the vicinity, without being too conspicuous, to give me time to issue orders. There's a brasserie on Place Dauphine where you'll be left alone.'

'Give me my coat.'

He seemed wearier than when he had come in, because he was no longer living on his nerves.

'And I think you should also find a room in the first hotel you come to and get some sleep.'

'I wouldn't be able to sleep.'

In the doorway, he turned.

'What are they going to do with her?'

Maigret understood.

'If nobody claims the body . . .' he began.

'Am I allowed to claim it?'

'If there's no family . . .'

'Will you tell me how to go about it?'

He wanted to give Lulu a decent funeral. Their friends from the dance hall and the Barbès district would probably follow the hearse.

Maigret watched his weary figure move away down the long corridor. He slowly closed the door, stood motionless for a while in the middle of his office and at last headed for the inspectors' room.

7.

It was about six o'clock when the car from the Police Judiciaire stopped on Avenue Carnot, outside the building where the Gouins lived but at the pavement opposite, the front of it pointing towards the Ternes neighbourhood. Night had fallen early: that day, there had not been any more sunshine than the three previous days.

The lights were on in the concierge's lodge. They were also on at the Gouins' on the fourth floor, in the left-hand part of the apartment. Here and there, other windows were lit.

Some apartments were temporarily unoccupied. The Ottrebons, for example, Belgians who were in high finance, were in Egypt for the winter. The Count of Tavera and his family, who lived on the second floor, spent the hunting season in their chateau somewhere to the south of the Loire.

Wedged into the back of the car, wrapped in his overcoat, with his pipe sticking out from his turned-up collar, Maigret did not move. He appeared to be in such a bad mood that after a few minutes the driver had taken a newspaper from his pocket and murmured:

'Do you mind?'

It was a wonder he could read without any more light than the reflected glow of a streetlamp.

Maigret had had the same air all afternoon. It wasn't a bad mood strictly speaking, his colleagues knew that, but the effect was the same, and the word had been passed around Quai des Orfèvres not to disturb him.

He had hardly left his office, except to emerge two or three times into the inspectors' room, where he looked at them with big eyes as if he had forgotten what he had come in for.

He had dealt with some long-pending files with as much ardour as if they had suddenly become really urgent. At about 4.30, he had made his first call to the American hospital in Neuilly.

'Is Professor Gouin operating at the moment?'

'Yes. He'll be at least another hour. Who shall I say called?'

He had hung up, reread the report that Janvier had drawn up on the tenants of the building and the answers he had been given. Nobody had heard the gunshot. On the same floor as Louise Filon, on the left-hand side, lived a certain Madame Mettetal, a widow, still young, who had been at the theatre on Monday evening. On the floor below, the Crémieux had given a dinner party for ten people which, by the time it ended, had been really boisterous.

Maigret had worked on another case and made a few unimportant phone calls.

At 5.30, when he had called Neuilly again, he had been told that the operation had just ended and that the professor was getting dressed. That was when he had taken the car.

There were few people passing on the pavements of Avenue Carnot, and not many cars on the street. Over the driver's shoulder, he could read a headline on the front page of the newspaper:

Pierrot the Musician released

It was he who had informed the reporters, in accordance with his promise. The clock on the dashboard, which let out a faint light, showed 6.20. If there had been a bistro closer, he would have had a drink, and he was sorry now that he had not stopped on the way.

It was not until 6.50 that a taxi stopped outside the building. Étienne Gouin was the first to get out and stand motionless on the pavement for a moment, while his assistant emerged in her turn from the car.

He was near a streetlamp and his figure stood out against the light. He must have been half a head taller than Maigret and was almost as broad-shouldered. It was hard to judge his build, because of his loose overcoat, which seemed too big for him and much longer than was the fashion that year. He couldn't have been unduly bothered about his appearance, and his hat was placed just anyhow on his head.

Standing there, he gave the impression of a fat man who had got thinner and retained only a strong frame.

He was waiting without any impatience, staring absently at a point in space, while the young woman took money from her bag to pay the driver. Then, as the taxi drove off, he stood listening to what she was telling him. She was presumably reminding him of his appointments the following day before she left.

She walked with him as far as the entrance, where she handed him the dark leather briefcase she had been holding in her hand and watched him enter the lift before setting off in the direction of the Ternes.

'Follow her.'

'Right, chief.'

The car only had to glide down the sloping avenue. Lucile Decaux was walking quickly, without turning. She was short, brown-haired and, as far as could be judged, plump. She turned the corner into Rue des Acacias and went straight into a pork butcher's, then into the bakery next door and finally, after about a hundred metres, into a dilapidated-looking building.

Maigret sat in the car for about ten more minutes. Then he went into the building in his turn and spoke to the concierge, whose lodge was of a different class from the one on Avenue Carnot, cluttered with an adult's bed and a child's cot.

'Mademoiselle Decaux?'

'Fourth floor on the right. She just got home.'

There was no lift. On the fourth floor, he rang a bell and heard steps inside.

'Who's there?' a voice asked from behind the door.

'Detective Chief Inspector Maigret.'

'One moment, please.'

The voice was neither surprised nor frightened. Before opening, she went to another room and took a few moments to come back: Maigret understood why when the door opened and he saw her in a dressing gown, her feet in slippers.

'Come in,' she said, looking at him curiously.

The apartment, consisting of three rooms and a kitchen, was extremely clean, the wooden floor so highly polished you could have slid on it as if on a skating rink. He was shown into the living room, which was more like a kind of studio, with a divan covered in a striped cloth, lots of books in cases, a gramophone and shelves full of records. Above the fireplace, where the young woman had just lighted some logs, was a framed photograph of Étienne Gouin.

'Do you mind if I take my coat off?'

'Please do. I was just making myself comfortable when you rang the bell.'

She wasn't pretty. Her features were irregular, her lips too thick, but she seemed to have a pleasant body.

'Am I stopping you from having your dinner?'

'It doesn't matter. Please sit down.'

She pointed to an armchair. She herself settled on the edge of the divan, pulling the hem of her dressing gown down over her bare legs.

She didn't ask him any questions, merely observed him the way some people observe a famous person they at last see in the flesh.

'I preferred not to disturb you at the hospital.'

'You'd have found that difficult, because I was in the operating theatre.'

'Are you usually present at the professor's operations?'

'Always.'

'How long has that been the case?'

'Ten years. Before that, I was his student.'

'Are you a doctor?'

'Yes.'

'May I ask how old you are?'

'I'm thirty-six.'

She was answering his questions without any hesitation, in a fairly neutral voice, but he nevertheless had the impression of a certain mistrust, perhaps a certain hostility.

'I'm here to clarify a few points of detail. As I'm sure you know, in an investigation like the one I'm conducting, everything has to be checked.'

She was waiting for the question.

'On Monday evening, unless I'm mistaken, you went to fetch your boss from Avenue Carnot just before eight.'

'That's right. I hailed a taxi and phoned the professor from the concierge's lodge to let him know I was waiting for him downstairs.'

'Is that your usual procedure?'

'Yes. I only go up when there's work in the office, or documents to take.'

'Where were you while the professor was coming down?'

'By the door of the lift.'

'So you know he stopped on the way down?'

'He stopped for a few minutes on the third floor. I assume you're aware of that?'

'Yes, I am.'

'Why haven't you asked the professor himself that question?'

He preferred not to answer.

'Did he behave just like the other evenings? Or did he seem worried?'

'Only about his patient's condition.'

'Did he say anything on the way to the hospital?'

'He doesn't talk a lot.'

'You must have got to Cochin a few minutes after eight. What happened then?'

'We went straight to the patient's room along with the intern on duty.'

'Did you spend the whole evening there?'

'No. The professor stayed in the room for about half an hour, watching out for certain reactions that didn't come. I told him he ought to get some rest.'

'What time was it when he went up to the fourth floor?'

'I know you already asked these questions at the hospital.'

'Was it the head nurse of the department who told you that?'

'It doesn't matter.'

'What time was it?'

'It wasn't yet nine.'

'You didn't go up with him?'

'I stayed with the patient. It was a child.'

'I know. What time did the professor come back down?'

'I went up at about eleven to tell him that what he was expecting to happen had happened.'

'Did you go into the room where he was lying down?'

'Yes.'

'Was he dressed?'

'At the hospital, he usually lies down fully dressed. He had simply taken off his jacket and loosened his tie.'

'So you spent all the time between half past eight and eleven at the patient's bedside. Which means it would have been possible for your boss to go back downstairs and leave the hospital without your knowing.'

She must have been expecting this, because he had asked the same question in Cochin and they must have told her, and yet he saw her chest rising more rapidly. Had she prepared her answer?

'It would have been impossible, because I went upstairs at a quarter past ten to see if he needed anything.'

Maigret, who was looking her in the eyes, said without raising his voice, and with a great deal of gentleness in his tone:

'You're lying, aren't you?'

'Why do you say that?'

'Because I sense that you're lying. Listen, Mademoiselle Decaux, it's easy for me to reconstruct your actions at the hospital. I can do it right now. Even if you've taught the staff well, there'll be someone who'll feel uneasy and admit the truth. You didn't go upstairs until eleven.'

'The professor didn't leave the hospital.'

'How do you know that?'

'Because I know him better than anyone.'

She pointed to the evening newspaper on a side table.

'I found that on a table in Neuilly and read it. Why did you release that young man?'

She meant Pierrot. From where he was sitting, he could read the name upside down.

'Are you so sure he didn't do it?'

'I'm not sure of anything.'

'But you suspect the professor of killing that girl.'

Instead of answering her question, he asked:

'Did you know her?'

'You forget I'm Monsieur Gouin's assistant. I was present when he operated on her.'

'Did you dislike her?'

'I had no reason to dislike her.'

As he had his pipe in his hand, she said:

'You can smoke. It doesn't bother me.'

'Is it correct to say that the relationship between the professor and you was more intimate than purely professional?'

'They told you that, too, did they?'

She smiled, with a certain condescension.

'Are you very bourgeois, Monsieur Maigret?'

'That depends on what you mean by that.'

'I'm trying to find out if you have fixed ideas about conventional morality.'

'I've been in the police force for nearly thirty-five years, my dear.'

'In that case, don't speak about intimate relationships. Yes, we've had an intimate relationship – our relationship as colleagues. The rest is of no importance.'

'Does that mean there's no love between you?'

'Certainly not in the sense you mean it. I admire Professor Gouin more than anyone else in the world. I try to help him as best I can. For ten hours, twelve hours a day, often more, I'm at his side, and it's become such a normal thing for both of us that sometimes he doesn't even notice. We often spend the whole night together waiting for particular symptoms to manifest themselves in a patient. When he operates in the provinces or abroad, I go with him. In the street, I pay his taxi fares and I'm the one who reminds him of his appointments, just as I'm the one who phones his wife to say that he won't be home.

'A long time ago, right at the beginning, things happened between us, the kind of things that normally happen between a man and a woman who find themselves in frequent contact.

'It didn't mean anything to him. He's done the same thing with the nurses and with many others.'

'Didn't it mean anything to you either?'

'Nothing at all.'

She was looking him straight in the eyes, as if challenging him to contradict her.

'Have you ever been in love?'

'With whom?'

'With anyone. With the professor.'

'Not in the way you mean it.'

'But you've devoted your life to him?'

'Yes.'

'Was it he who chose you as his assistant when you qualified?'

'It was I who put myself forward. It was something I'd been thinking about ever since I started attending his classes.'

'You said that at the beginning certain things happened between you. Am I to understand they don't happen any more?'

'You're an excellent father confessor, Monsieur Maigret. They still happen every now and again.'

'In your apartment?'

'He's never set foot here. I don't see him climbing the four floors to get here.'

'At the hospital?'

'Sometimes. Sometimes also in his apartment. You're forgetting I'm also his secretary and that we often spend part of the day on Avenue Carnot.'

'Do you know his wife well?'

'We see each other almost every day.'

'How would you describe your relationship with her?'

He had the impression that a harder look came into Lucile Decaux's eyes.

'I'm indifferent to her,' she said.

'Is that mutual?'

'What is it you want me to tell you?'

'The truth.'

'Let's just say that Madame Gouin looks at me the same way she looks at her servants. I suppose she has to make an effort to convince herself that she's the professor's wife. Have you met her?'

Once again, Maigret avoided answering.

'Why did your boss marry her?'

'So as not to be alone, I suppose.'

'That was before you became his assistant, wasn't it?'

'Several years earlier.'

'Does he get on well with her?'

'He's not the kind of man who quarrels with anyone, and he has a remarkable ability to ignore people.'

'Does he ignore his wife?'

'He has some of his meals with her.'

'Is that all?'

'As far as I know.'

'Why do you think she married him?'

'She was just an ordinary nurse, don't forget. The professor is said to be a rich man.'

'Is he?'

'He earns a lot of money. He doesn't care about things like that.'

'But he has a considerable fortune?'

She nodded and uncrossed her legs, not forgetting to pull down on the hem of her dressing gown.

'In short, in your opinion, he isn't happy in his marriage.'

'That's not quite correct. His wife couldn't make him unhappy.'

'What about Lulu?'

'Nor could Lulu, that's my belief.'

'If he wasn't in love with her, how do you explain the fact that for more than two years—'

'I can't explain it. You'll have to figure it out for yourself.'

'Someone told me she'd got under his skin.'

'Who told you that?'

'Isn't it true?'

'It is and it isn't. She'd become something that belonged to him.'

'But he wouldn't have got a divorce in order to marry her?'

She looked at him in astonishment.

'No, of course not! He would never have put himself through the complication of a divorce.'

'Even to marry you?'

'He's never thought about it.'

'And you?'

She blushed.

'Neither have I. What would I have gained by it? On the contrary, I would have lost on the deal. You see, I've always had the best of him, and still have. He does hardly anything without me. I take part in his work. I read his books as he writes them and often I'm the one who does the research. He won't cross Paris by taxi without me at his side.'

'Is he afraid of dying suddenly?'

'Why do you ask that?'

She seemed surprised at Maigret's insight.

'It's been true for a few years now, pretty much ever since he discovered that he has a weak heart. At the time, he consulted several of his colleagues. You may not know this, but most doctors are more frightened by illness than their patients.'

'I do know that.'

'He's never said anything to me about it, but gradually he's got into the habit of never being on his own.'

'If he had an attack, in a taxi, say, what could you do?'

'Not very much. But I understand him.'

'So basically, it's the thought of dying alone that frightens him.'

'Why exactly have you come to see me, inspector?'

'Perhaps in order not to disturb your boss needlessly. His mistress was killed on Monday evening.'

'I don't like that word. It's inaccurate.'

'I use it in the meaning that's usually given to it. Physically speaking, Gouin could have committed the murder. As you yourself admitted earlier, he was alone on the fourth floor of the hospital from a quarter to nine until eleven. There was nothing to stop him going downstairs and getting a ride to Avenue Carnot.'

'First of all, if you knew him, the idea would never even occur to you that he could kill someone.'

'On the contrary!' he retorted.

He was so categorical that she looked at him with astonishment, without thinking of objecting.

'What do you mean?'

'You admit that his work, his career – his scientific research, his teaching, his medical activities, whatever – is the only thing that matters to him.'

'To an extent.'

'To a much greater extent than anyone else I've ever met. Someone used about him the words "force of nature".'

This time, she didn't ask who.

'Forces of nature don't care about the damage they cause. If, for one reason or another, Lulu had become a threat to his activities—'

'How could she have threatened the professor's activities?'

'You know she was pregnant?'

'What difference would that have made?'

She didn't seem surprised.

'So you knew?'

'The professor told me.'

'When?'

'Last Saturday.'

'Are you certain that he told you on Saturday?'

'Absolutely. We were in the taxi, coming back from the hospital. He told me, just as he tells me lots of things, without making much of it, as if he was talking to himself, "I think Louise is pregnant."'

'How did he seem?'

'Fine. Quite ironic, the way he usually is. You see, there are lots of things people think are important and he doesn't.'

'What surprises me is that he could have talked to you about it on Saturday, when it wasn't until about six on Monday evening that Lulu herself found out.'

'You forget that he's a doctor and that he was sleeping with her.'

'You think he told his wife, too.'

'It's unlikely.'

'What if Louise Filon had got it into her head to get him to marry her?'

'I doubt the thought ever crossed her mind. And, even if it had, he wouldn't have killed her. You're barking up the wrong tree, inspector. I'm not claiming you let the real culprit go. I don't see why that Pierrot would have killed the girl either.'

'Out of love, if she'd threatened not to see him again.'

She shrugged.

'That's going a bit far.'

'What do you think?'

'I have no reason to think anything.'

He stood up to empty his pipe in the fireplace and, automatically, as if he were in his own home, picked up the tongs to arrange the logs.

'Are you thinking about his wife?' he asked in a casual tone, with his back turned.

'I'm not thinking about anyone.'

'You don't like her?'

How could she have liked her? Germaine Gouin was a mere nurse, a fisherman's daughter, who overnight had become the lawful wedded wife of the professor while she, Lucile Decaux, who had devoted her life to him and was quite capable of helping him in his work, was only his assistant. Every evening, when they got back from the hospital, she would get out of the taxi with him, but only to say goodnight in the doorway of his building and go home to her apartment in Rue des Acacias while he went upstairs to his wife.

'Do you suspect her, Mademoiselle Decaux?'

'I never said that.'

'But you think it?'

'I think you're only too eager to pry into my boss's actions during Monday evening, but that you don't care about hers.'

'How do you know that?'

'Have you spoken to her?'

'I've at least learned, never mind how, that she spent the evening with her sister. Do you know Antoinette?'

'Not personally. The professor has told me about her.'

'He doesn't like her?'

'It's she who hates him. He told me once that whenever they happen to meet, he always expects her to spit in his face.'

'Do you know anything else about Madame Gouin?'

'Nothing!' she said curtly.

'Does she have a lover?'

'Not as far as I know. But it's none of my business anyway.'

'Is she the kind of woman who'd let her husband take the blame if she herself was guilty?'

She said nothing.

Maigret couldn't help smiling. 'Admit you wouldn't be upset if she was the one who killed Lulu and we found out.'

'The one thing I know for sure is that the professor didn't kill her.'

'Did he mention the murder to you?'

'Not on the Tuesday morning. He didn't yet know. In the afternoon, he told me casually that the police would probably be phoning to ask to see him.'

'And since then?'

'He hasn't mentioned it again.'

'Didn't Louise's death affect him?'

'If he was upset, he hasn't shown it. He's the same as usual.'

'I don't suppose you have anything else to tell me? Did he ever talk to you about Pierre Eyraud, the musician?'

'Never.'

'Did it ever occur to you that he might be jealous of him?'

'He's not the kind of man to be jealous of anybody.'

'I'm grateful to you, my dear, and I'm sorry I delayed your dinner. If you happen to remember anything interesting, don't hesitate to phone me.'

'Aren't you going to see my boss?'

'I don't know yet. Is he at home this evening?'

'It's his only free evening of the week.'

'How will he spend it?'

'Working, as usual. He has the proofs of his book to go through.'

Maigret put on his overcoat with a sigh.

'You're a strange girl,' he murmured as if to himself.

'There's nothing remarkable about me.'

'Good evening.'

'Good evening, Monsieur Maigret.'

She walked him out on to the landing and watched him go downstairs. Outside, the black car stood waiting. The driver opened the door.

He almost gave him the address on Avenue Carnot. Sooner or later he'd have to make up his mind to talk directly to Gouin. Why did he keep putting it off? He seemed to be circling around him without daring to move in closer, as if the professor's personality overawed him.

'To Quai des Orfèvres!'

At this hour, Étienne Gouin must be in the middle of dinner with his wife. In passing, Maigret saw that there was no light in the right-hand part of the apartment.

There was at least one point on which the assistant had been mistaken. Contrary to what she had asserted, Gouin's conjugal relations were less neutral than she thought. Lucile Decaux claimed that her boss didn't talk about his personal affairs with his wife. But as it happened, Madame Gouin had given Maigret details she could only have got from her husband.

Had he also told her that he thought Lulu was pregnant?

He had the driver stop the car a little further along the avenue, outside the bistro where he had stopped once for a toddy. It was less cold this evening, and he ordered something else, a marc, even though it wasn't the hour for neat alcohol, simply because it was what he had drunk the previous day. It was a habit they teased him about at Quai des Orfèvres. If he started a case with calvados, for example, it was with calvados that he continued it, so that there were cases accompanied by beer, others by red wine, there had even been some where whisky was the drink of choice.

He was about to phone the office to ask if there was any news and have himself driven straight home. It was only because there was someone in the phone booth that he changed his mind.

He didn't speak on the way.

'Do you still need me?' the driver asked, once they were in the courtyard of the Police Judiciaire.

'You can take me back to Boulevard Richard-Lenoir in a few minutes. Unless you've finished your shift.'

'I don't finish until eight.'

He went upstairs and switched the light on in his office, whose second door opened immediately to admit Lucas.

'Inspector Janin called. He's upset that nobody told him Pierrot had been found.'

Everyone had forgotten about Janin, who had continued to search the La Chapelle neighbourhood until he had learned from the newspapers that the musician had been questioned by Maigret and released.

'He's asking if he still needs to keep an eye on him.'

'There's no point any more. Anything else?'

Lucas was just opening his mouth when the telephone rang. Maigret picked up the receiver.

'Detective Chief Inspector Maigret speaking,' he said with a frown.

Immediately, Lucas realized it was important.

'This is Étienne Gouin,' said the voice at the other end.

'I'm listening.'

'I understand you've just questioned my assistant.'

Lucile Decaux had phoned her boss to let him know.

'That's correct,' Maigret said.

'If you require information about me, it would have struck me as more proper for you to address me directly.'

Lucas had the impression that Maigret was losing a little of his composure and was making an effort to regain it.

'That's a matter of judgement,' he replied quite curtly. 'You know where I live.'

'Yes, of course. I'll come and see you.'

There was a silence at the other end of the line. Maigret could vaguely hear a woman's voice. It was probably Madame Gouin saying something to her husband.

'When?' the professor asked.

'In an hour, an hour and a half. I haven't had dinner yet.'

'I'll be waiting.'

He hung up.

'The professor?' Lucas asked.

Maigret nodded.

'What does he want?'

'He wants to be questioned. Are you free?'

'To go over there with you?'

'Yes. But we'll have a bite to eat before that.'

They did so on Place Dauphine, at the table where the inspector had lunched and dined so many times that it was called Maigret's table.

He didn't say a word throughout the meal.

8.

Maigret had questioned thousands, tens of thousands of people in the course of his career, some occupying important positions, others who were more famous for their wealth and others still who were considered the most intelligent of international criminals.

Yet he attached an importance to this interrogation he had attached to no previous interrogation, and it wasn't Gouin's social position that overawed him, or his worldwide fame.

He was well aware that Lucas, since the beginning of the case, had been wondering why he didn't just go and ask the professor a few specific questions. Even now, good old Lucas was disconcerted by his chief's mood.

The truth was something Maigret couldn't admit to him, or to anybody, not even to his wife. Frankly, he didn't dare formulate it clearly to himself in his own mind.

What he knew of Gouin, what he had learned about him, impressed him, it was true. But for a reason that nobody would have been likely to guess.

Like the professor, Maigret had been born in a village in the centre of France and, like him, he had had to fend for himself at an early age.

Maigret had even started studying medicine. If he had been able to continue, he probably wouldn't have become a surgeon, lacking the necessary manual dexterity, but he nevertheless had the impression that there were a number of things that he and Lulu's lover had in common.

It was pride on his part, and that was why he preferred not to think about it. They both, it seemed to him, had an almost equal knowledge of men and life.

Not the same knowledge, and above all not the same reactions. They were rather like opposites, but equal opposites.

What he knew about Gouin he had learned from the words and attitudes of five different women. Otherwise, all he had seen of him was his shadowy figure on the pavement of Avenue Carnot and a photograph above a fireplace, and the most revealing incident was no doubt the brief account that Janvier had given him on the telephone of the professor's appearance in Louise Filon's apartment.

He was going to find out if he had been wrong. He had prepared himself as much as possible and the reason he was taking Lucas was not because he needed his help, but to give a more official character to the interview – perhaps, when it came down to it, to remind himself that he was going to Avenue Carnot in his capacity as a detective chief inspector of the Police Judiciaire and not as a man interested in another man.

He had drunk wine with his meal. Then, when the waiter had come and asked him if he would like any spirits, he had ordered an old marc from Burgundy, so that by the time he got into the car he felt warm inside.

Avenue Carnot was quiet and deserted, with soft lights behind the windows of the apartments. As he passed the lodge, he had the feeling the concierge watched him walk by with an air of reproach.

The two men took the lift. Around them, the building was silent, withdrawn into itself and its secrets.

It was 8.40 when Maigret pulled the polished brass handle, which activated an electric bell. Footsteps were heard inside, and a fairly young and rather pretty chambermaid, wearing a smart apron over her black uniform, opened the door and said:

'If you'd like to take your coats off . . .'

He had wondered if Gouin would receive them in the drawing room, in the family part of the apartment, so to speak. He didn't have the answer immediately. The maid hung the clothes in a wardrobe, left the visitors in the hall and disappeared.

She did not return, but before long Gouin appeared and came towards them. He seemed taller and thinner here. Barely looking at them, he murmured:

'If you'd like to come this way . . .'

He walked in front of them down a corridor that led to the library. The walls were almost entirely covered in bound books. The lighting was soft, and logs burned in a fireplace much larger than the one in Lucile Decaux's apartment.

'Please sit down.'

He pointed to some armchairs and chose one for himself. None of this mattered. Neither had yet looked at each other. Lucas, who felt superfluous, was all the more ill at ease because the armchair was too deep for his short legs, and he was sitting closest to the fire.

'I was expecting you to come alone.'

Maigret introduced his colleague. 'I brought Sergeant Lucas, who'll take notes.'

It was at that moment that their eyes met for the first time, and Maigret saw something like a reproach in the professor's gaze. Was there also – although he couldn't be sure – a degree of disappointment? It was hard to say because, on the surface, Gouin was fairly ordinary. There are theatre actors, especially singing basses, who have tall bony bodies like that, faces with strongly drawn features, bags under their eyes.

The pupils were small and clear, without any particular gleam, and yet there was an uncommon weight in his gaze.

Maigret would have sworn, as this gaze came to rest on him, that Gouin was as curious about him as he was about the professor.

Did he, too, find Maigret more commonplace than the image of him he had built up?

Lucas had taken a notebook and a pencil from his pocket to disguise his unease.

It was impossible to know yet what tone the interview would assume, and Maigret was careful to be silent and wait.

'Don't you think, Monsieur Maigret, that it would have been more logical to address me directly rather than go and bother that poor girl?'

He was speaking naturally, in a monotonous voice, as if he were saying banal things.

'Do you mean Mademoiselle Decaux? She didn't seem to me the least bit embarrassed. I assume she phoned you as soon as I left her to bring you up to date?'

'She repeated to me your questions and her answers. She imagined it was important. Women have a constant need to be convinced of their own importance.'

'Lucile Decaux is your closest colleague, isn't she?'

'She's my assistant.'

'Isn't she also your secretary?'

'Yes, she is. In fact, as I'm sure she told you, she follows me everywhere I go. It gives her the impression she plays a vital role in my life.'

'Is she in love with you?'

'As she would be of any employer, provided he was famous.'

'She struck me as devoted, to the point, for example, that she'd make a false statement, if necessary, in order to get you out of trouble.'

'She'd do so without any hesitation. My wife has also been in contact with you.'

'Did she tell you?'

'Just like Lucile, she reported your conversation in the minutest detail.'

He was speaking about his wife in the same detached tone he had assumed to talk about his assistant. There was no warmth in his voice. He was observing facts, relating them, without granting them any sentimental value.

The little people who approached him must have been delighted with his simplicity, and indeed there was no affectation about him, he was not in the least concerned about the effect he produced on others.

It is rare to encounter people who do not play a role, even when they are alone. Most men feel the need to watch themselves living, to listen to themselves speaking.

Not Gouin. He was himself, fully himself, and he did not bother to hide his feelings.

When he had spoken about Lucile Decaux, his words and attitude seemed to say:

'What she takes for devotion is only a kind of vanity, the need to think herself exceptional. Any of my female students would do exactly the same. She makes her life interesting and no doubt imagines that I owe her a debt of gratitude.'

The only reason he didn't say this was because he judged Maigret capable of understanding. He was talking to him as an equal.

'I haven't yet told you why I phoned you this evening and asked you to come. Mind you, I was keen to meet you anyway.'

He was a man, and he was sincere. He hadn't taken his eyes off Maigret since they had been face to face, and he was making no attempt to conceal it; he was examining him like a human specimen he wanted to get to know.

'My wife and I were having dinner when I received a telephone call. It was from someone you already know, a certain Madame Brault, who did the cleaning for Louise.'

He didn't say Lulu, but Louise. He spoke about her as simply as he spoke about the others, knowing perfectly well that it was superfluous to provide explanations.

'Madame Brault has got it into her head that she has something in her possession she can use to blackmail me. She didn't beat about the bush, although I didn't understand what she was talking about at first. She said, "I have the gun, Monsieur Gouin." My first thought was to wonder what gun she meant.'

'Will you allow me a question?'

'Go ahead.'

'Have you ever met Madame Brault?'

'I don't think so. Louise told me about her. She knew her before she moved in here. Apparently she's a strange character, who's been in prison several times. As she only worked in the apartment in the mornings and I've hardly ever had occasion to go there at that time, I don't recall ever having seen her. I suppose I might have passed her on the stairs.'

'You can go on.'

'Anyway, she told me that when she went into the living room on Tuesday morning, she found the gun on the table and—'

'Did she say specifically "on the table"?'

'Yes. She added that she hid it in a potted plant out on the landing. Your men must have searched inside the apartment without thinking of looking outside.'

'That was shrewd of her.'

'Anyway, she now apparently has that gun and would be willing to give it back to me for a large sum of money.'

'Give it *back* to you?'

'It's my gun.'

'How do you know?'

'She described it to me, including the serial number.'

'Have you had this weapon a long time?'

'Eight or nine years. I'd gone to Belgium to perform an operation. I travelled more in those days than I do now. I've even sometimes been called as far afield as the United States and India. My wife had often told me she was afraid of being alone in the apartment for several days, sometimes several weeks. In the hotel where I was staying in Liège, some locally manufactured weapons were on display in a case. I got the idea of buying a little automatic. I should add that I didn't declare it to customs.'

Maigret smiled.

'What room was it in?'

'In a drawer in my office. That was where I last saw it, a few months ago. I've never used it. I'd completely forgotten about it when I got that phone call.'

'What did you tell Madame Brault?'

'That I'd give her an answer.'

'When?'

'Probably this evening. That was when I called you.'

'Would you go over there, Lucas? Do you have the address?'

'Yes, chief.'

Lucas looked delighted to escape the heavy atmosphere of the room, because, although the two men were talking quietly and in an apparently matter-of-fact way, there was an underlying tension in the air.

'Will you be able to find your coat? Would you like me to ring for the maid?'

'I'll find it.'

Once the door was closed, they fell silent for a moment. It was Maigret who broke the silence.

'Does your wife know?'

'About Madame Brault's attempt at blackmail?'

'Yes.'

'She heard what I was answering on the phone, because I took the call in the dining room. I filled her in on the rest.'

'What was her reaction?'

'She advised me to give in.'

'Did you wonder why?'

'You see, Monsieur Maigret, whether it's my wife, Lucile Decaux or any other woman, they feel an intense satisfaction in convincing themselves that they're devoted to me. They compete with one another in helping and protecting me.'

He was speaking without any irony – without any resentment either. He was dissecting their state of mind with the same detachment he would have used to dissect a corpse.

'Why do you think my wife felt the need to speak to you? To give herself the role of the wife protecting her husband's peace and quiet, and his work.'

'Isn't that the case?'

He looked at Maigret without answering.

'Your wife, professor, struck me as unusually understanding towards you.'

'She does claim not to be jealous.'

'Is it only a claim?'

'That depends on the meaning you give the word "jealous". There's no doubt she doesn't care who I sleep with.'

'Even with Louise Filon?'

'Not at first. Don't forget that Germaine was just an ordinary nurse before she became Madame Gouin overnight.'

'Did you love her?'

'No.'

'Why did you marry her?'

'To have someone in the house. The old woman who took care of me didn't have long to live. I don't like being alone, Monsieur Maigret. I don't know if you're familiar with that feeling?'

'Perhaps you also prefer it when the people around you owe you everything?'

He didn't object. On the contrary, the remark seemed to please him.

'In a way, yes.'

'Is that why you chose a girl from a humble background?'

'The others exasperate me.'

'Did she know what to expect when she married you?'

'She knew exactly what to expect.'

'When did she start to be unpleasant?'

'She's never been unpleasant. You've seen her. She's perfect, takes marvellous care of the apartment, never insists that I go out in the evening or that we invite friends for dinner.'

'If I understand correctly, she spends her days waiting for you.'

'Pretty much. She's content with being Madame Gouin and knowing that one day she'll be the Widow Gouin.'

'Do you think she's self-interested?'

'Let's just say she won't be upset to get her hands on the fortune I'll leave her. For the moment, I'd bet you anything she's listening at the door. She was upset when I called you. She would have preferred me to receive you in the drawing room, in her presence.'

He had not lowered his voice when he said that Germaine was listening behind the door, and Maigret could have sworn he heard a slight noise in the next room.

'According to her, she was the one who suggested you bring Louise Filon here.'

'That's true. I hadn't thought of it. I didn't even know an apartment was free.'

'Didn't that arrangement strike you as strange?'

'Why?' The question surprised him.

'Did you love Louise?'

'Listen, Monsieur Maigret, that's the second time you've used that word. In medicine, we don't know it.'

'Did you need her?'

'Physically, yes. Do I have to explain myself? I'm sixty-two years old.'

'I know.'

'That says it all.'

'Weren't you jealous of Pierrot?'

'I'd have preferred it if he didn't exist.'

As in Lucile Decaux's apartment, Maigret stood up to go and put straight a log that had collapsed. He was thirsty. The professor hadn't thought of offering him a drink. His mouth was furry from the marc he had had after dinner, and he hadn't stopped smoking.

'Did you ever meet him?' he asked.

'Who?'

'Pierrot.'

'Once. Usually, they both made sure it didn't happen.'

'What were Lulu's feelings towards you?'

'What should they have been? I suppose you know her history. Of course, she told me she was grateful, she was fond of me. The truth is simpler. She had no desire to fall back into poverty. You must know that. People who've really been hungry, who've been poor in the grimmest sense of the word and who, in one way or another, have escaped, would do anything not to fall back into their old lives.'

It was true. Maigret knew it as well as anyone.

'Did she love Pierrot?'

'How fond of that word you are!' the professor sighed, resigned. 'She had to have something sentimental in her life. She also had to make problems for herself. I said earlier that women need to feel important. I suppose that's why they complicate their lives, ask themselves questions, always imagine that they have a choice.'

'What kind of choice?' Maigret asked with a hint of a smile, to force his interlocutor to be more specific.

'Louise imagined she had a choice between her musician and me.'

'Didn't she?'

'In actual fact, no. I've told you why.'

'Did she ever threaten to leave you?'

'She sometimes claimed she was thinking about it.'

'Weren't you afraid it would happen?'

'No.'

'Didn't she ever try to get you to marry her?'

'She didn't aim that high. I'm convinced she would have been a little terrified to become Madame Gouin. What she needed was security. A nice warm apartment, three meals a day, decent clothes.'

'What would have happened if you'd died?'

'I took out a life insurance policy in her name.'

'Did you also take one out in Lucile Decaux's name?'

'No. There's no point. When I'm dead, she'll latch on to my successor just as she latched on to me, and nothing will have changed in her life.'

The ringing of the telephone interrupted them. Gouin was about to stand up to answer, then stopped.

'That must be your inspector.'

It was indeed Lucas, phoning from the Batignolles police station, the closest to Désirée Brault's apartment.

'I have the gun, chief. She claimed at first she didn't know what I was talking about.'

'What have you done with her?'

'She's here with me.'

'Have her taken to headquarters. Where did she find the gun?'

'She still claims it was on the table.'

'Why did she conclude it belonged to the professor?'

'According to her, it's obvious. She isn't going into details. She's furious. She tried to scratch me. What does he say?'

'Nothing definite yet. We're chatting.'

'Shall I join you?'

'Go to the lab first to make sure there are no prints on the automatic. That'll give you a chance to take your prisoner there.'

'All right, chief,' Lucas sighed unenthusiastically.

It was only then that Gouin thought of offering Maigret a drink.

'Would you like a glass of brandy?'

'Gladly.'

He pushed a button. The maid who had admitted Maigret and Lucas soon appeared.

'The brandy!'

They did not speak as they waited for her. When she came back, there was only one glass on the tray.

'Please excuse me, but I never drink,' the professor said, letting Maigret serve himself.

It wasn't out of virtue, probably not for health reasons either, but because he didn't need it.

9.

Maigret took his time. His glass in his hand, he was looking at the professor's face, while the professor, for his part, looked at him calmly.

'The concierge also owes you a debt of gratitude, doesn't she? If I'm not mistaken, you saved her son.'

'I don't expect gratitude from anyone.'

'Nevertheless she's devoted to you, and, like Lucile Decaux, would be ready to lie to get you out of an awkward situation.'

'Of course. It's always pleasant to think one's being heroic.'

'Don't you feel alone sometimes, in the world as you see it?'

'All human beings are alone, whatever they think. You just have to admit it and adjust to it.'

'I thought you hated solitude?'

'That's not the kind of solitude I meant. Let's say, if you prefer, that what distresses me is emptiness. I don't like to be alone in the apartment, or in the street, or in a car. It's about physical solitude rather than moral isolation.'

'Are you afraid of death?'

'I don't care about being dead. I hate death itself, with all it entails. In your profession, inspector, you've seen it almost as often as I have.'

He knew perfectly well that this was his weak point, that this fear of dying alone was the little touch of human cowardice that made him, in spite of everything, a man like any other. He wasn't ashamed of it.

'Since my last heart attack, I've almost always had someone with me. Medically, it wouldn't be any help. Nevertheless, strange as it may seem, any presence reassures me. Once when I was alone in the city and I felt slightly faint, I went into the first bar I came across.'

This was the moment that Maigret chose to ask the question he had been keeping in reserve for a long time.

'What was your reaction when you realized that Louise was pregnant?'

He seemed surprised, not that the subject should be brought up, but that it should be considered a possible problem.

'I didn't have any reaction,' he said simply.

'Didn't she tell you?'

'No. I assume she didn't yet know.'

'She found out at about six o'clock on Monday. You saw her after that. Didn't she say anything?'

'Only that she wasn't feeling well and was going to bed.'

'Did you think the child was yours?'

'I didn't think any such thing.'

'Have you ever had children?'

'Not as far as I know.'

'Have you ever wanted to?'

His reply shocked Maigret: for thirty years now, his greatest regret had been that he wasn't a father.

'*Why should I?*' the professor asked.

'Precisely!'

'What do you mean?'

'Nothing.'

'Some people, who have no serious interests in life, imagine that a child makes them important, useful in some way, makes them feel they'll be leaving something behind them. I'm not one of those people.'

'Don't you think that, given your age and her boy-friend's, Lulu would have assumed the child was his?'

'There's no scientific basis for that.'

'I'm talking about what she may have thought.'

'It's possible.'

'Wasn't that sufficient to make up her mind to leave you for Pierrot?'

He did not hesitate.

'No,' he replied, still like a man who is sure he possesses the truth. 'She would surely have told me the child was mine.'

'Would you have recognized the child as your own?'

'Why not?'

'Even if you had doubts that you were the father?'

'What difference does that make? One child is as good as any other.'

'Would you have married the mother?'

'I don't see why I should.'

'Don't you think she would have tried to get you to marry her?'

'If she had, she wouldn't have succeeded.'

'Because you don't want to leave your wife?'

'Simply because I find these complications ridiculous. I'm answering you frankly, because I think you're able to understand me.'

'Did you talk about it with your wife?'

'On Sunday afternoon, if I remember correctly. Yes, it was Sunday. I spent part of the afternoon at home.'

'Why did you tell her?'

'I told my assistant, too.'

'I know.'

'And?'

He was right to think that Maigret understood. There was something terribly arrogant, and at the same time tragic, in the way the professor spoke about those around him, especially the women. He took them all at face value, without the slightest illusion, asking of each only what she could give him. It was as if, to him, they were not much more than inanimate objects.

Nor did he take the trouble to keep silent in front of them. What would have been the point? He could think aloud, without worrying how they might react, let alone what they might be thinking or feeling.

'What did your wife say?'

'She asked me what I was planning to do.'

'Did you tell her you would recognize the child?'

He nodded.

'Didn't it occur to you this might upset her?'

'Perhaps.'

This time, Maigret suspected something in the other man that hadn't come through so far, or that he hadn't been able to spot. There was a secret satisfaction in the professor's voice as he said, '*Perhaps.*'

'So you did it deliberately?' he said sharply.

'Telling her, you mean?'

Maigret was sure that Gouin would have preferred not to smile, to remain impassive, but he couldn't help it, and, for the first time, his lips curled strangely.

'In other words, you were quite content to upset your wife, and your assistant.'

The way Gouin kept silent constituted an admission.

'Mightn't one or other of them have got it into their heads to get rid of Louise Filon?'

'It's an idea they must both have been fairly familiar with for a long time. They both hated Louise. I don't know anyone who hasn't wished for the death of another human being at some time or other. Only, people capable of putting their idea into practice are rare. Fortunately for you!'

It was all true. Which was what made this conversation so incredible. What the professor had said from the start was, when it came down to it, what Maigret himself thought. Their ideas about men and their motives weren't so different.

What was different was their attitude to the problem.

Gouin only used what Maigret would have called his cold reason. Whereas Maigret tried to . . .

He would have been hard put to define what it was he tried to do. Perhaps understanding people gave him a feeling that wasn't just pity, but a kind of affection.

Gouin looked at them from a great height.

Maigret put himself on the same level as them.

'Louise Filon was murdered,' he said slowly.

'That's a fact. Someone went all the way.'

'Have you wondered who?'

'That's your job, not mine.'

'Did it occur to you we might think it was you?'

'Of course. At that time I didn't yet know that my wife had spoken to you, and I was surprised you didn't come and question me. The concierge told me you knew about me.'

She, too! And Gouin accepted it as his due!

'You went to Cochin on Monday night, but you only stayed half an hour at your patient's bedside.'

'I went up to sleep in a room on the fourth floor that's kept at my disposal.'

'You were alone there, and there was nothing to stop you leaving the hospital without being seen, coming here by taxi and then going back to your room.'

'At what time, according to you, did these comings and goings take place?'

'It would have had to be between nine and eleven.'

'At what time was Pierre Eyraud in Louise's apartment?'

'At a quarter to ten.'

'So I would have had to kill Louise after that?'

Maigret nodded.

'Given the time it would have taken me to make the journey, I wouldn't have been back at the hospital between ten and half past.'

Maigret calculated mentally. The professor's argument was logical. And suddenly, Maigret looked disappointed.

Something wasn't happening as he had foreseen. He was expecting what was to come, barely listening to what his interlocutor was telling him.

'It so happens, Monsieur Maigret, that at five past ten a colleague of mine, Dr Lanvin, who had just examined a patient on the third floor, came upstairs to see me. He didn't trust his own diagnosis and asked me if I could come with him. I went down to the third floor. Neither my assistant nor the staff in my department could have told you that, because they didn't know.

'This isn't the testimony of a woman anxious to get me out of trouble, but of five or six people, including the patient, who'd never seen me before and probably doesn't even know my name.'

'I've never thought you killed Lulu.'

He deliberately called her by that name, which appeared to displease the professor. Maigret, too, had a desire to be cruel.

'I'd simply expected you to try to cover for the person who did kill her.'

Gouin took this in. A slight flush appeared on his cheeks, and for a moment he turned his eyes away from Maigret.

The doorbell rang. It was Lucas. The maid admitted him. He had a little package in his hand.

'No prints,' he said, unwrapping the gun and handing it to his chief.

He looked at both of them, surprised at the prevailing calm, surprised also to find them in exactly the same places, in the same poses, as if, while he'd been running about the city, time here had stood still.

'This is your gun, isn't it, Monsieur Gouin?'

It was a fancy weapon, with a nickel-plated barrel and a mother-of-pearl grip. If the shot hadn't been fired at close range, it probably would not have done much harm.

'There's a bullet missing from the magazine,' Lucas said. 'I phoned Gastine-Renette. He'll do the usual tests tomorrow. But for now he's convinced that this is the gun that was used on Monday.'

'I assume, Monsieur Gouin, that both your wife and your assistant had access to your desk drawer? It wasn't locked?'

'I never lock anything.'

That, too, was a kind of contempt for people. He had nothing to hide. He didn't care if anyone read his personal papers.

'You weren't surprised when you came home on Monday night to find your sister-in-law in the apartment?'

'She usually avoids me.'

'I think she hates you, doesn't she?'

'It's another way to make her life interesting.'

'Your wife told me her sister just happened to drop by because she was in the neighbourhood.'

'It's possible.'

'But when I questioned Antoinette, she told me her sister had phoned her and asked her to come over.'

Gouin was listening attentively, but it was impossible to detect any particular expression on his face. Sitting back in his armchair, his legs crossed, he kept his fingers together, and Maigret was struck by the length of those fingers, as slender as a pianist's.

'Sit down, Lucas.'

'Would you like me to ask for a drink for your inspector?'

Lucas refused with a gesture.

'There's another thing your wife stated that I need to check and I can only do so through you.'

The professor gave a sign that he was waiting.

'She said that some time ago you had a blackout while you were in Lulu's apartment.'

'That's true. A little exaggerated, but true.'

'Is it also correct that your mistress called your wife in a panic?'

Gouin seemed surprised.

'Who told you that?'

'Never mind. Is it the truth?'

'Not completely.'

'You do realize your answer is of great importance.'

'I realize it from the way you are asking the question, but I have no idea why. One night, I didn't feel well. I asked Louise to come up here and fetch a flask of medicine which was in my bathroom. She did so. My wife opened the door to her, because the servants were in bed, and their rooms are on the sixth floor. My wife, who was also in bed when Louise arrived, went to look for the flask.'

'Did they go down together?'

'Yes. Only, in the meantime the attack had passed, and I'd already left the downstairs apartment. In fact, I was just coming through the door when Louise and my wife appeared, both in their nightdresses.'

'Will you excuse me for a moment?'

Maigret said a few words in a low voice to Lucas, who left the room. Gouin didn't ask any questions, didn't appear surprised.

'Was the door wide open behind you?'

'It was slightly ajar.'

Maigret would have preferred him to lie. For an hour now, he had been hoping that Gouin would try to lie, but he was relentlessly honest.

'Are you sure?'

He was giving him a last chance.

'Absolutely.'

'As far as you know, has your wife ever been to see Lulu in the apartment on the third floor?'

'You don't know her.'

Hadn't Germaine Gouin asserted that it was the only opportunity she had had to see the inside of the apartment?

The fact was, she hadn't gone inside that night. Yet when she had come downstairs to meet Maigret, she hadn't looked around her with any curiosity, but had acted as if the place was familiar to her.

It was her second lie, added to which was the fact that she hadn't mentioned that Lulu was pregnant.

'Do you think she's still listening at the door?'

It was a pointless precaution on his part to have sent Lucas to take up position at the entrance to the apartment.

'I'm convinced of it . . .' the professor began.

And indeed the communicating door now opened. Madame Gouin took two steps forwards, just enough to be able to look her husband in the face, and never before had Maigret seen so much hate and contempt in human eyes. The professor did not turn away but absorbed the shock without flinching.

As for Maigret, he stood up.

'I'm obliged to arrest you, Madame Gouin.'

'I know,' she said, almost absently, still turned towards her husband.

'I assume you heard everything?'

'Yes.'

'Do you admit you killed Louise Filon?'

She nodded, and it looked for a moment as if she were about to throw herself like a fury at the professor, who still sustained her gaze.

'He knew it would happen,' she said at last in a staccato voice, while her chest rose and fell rapidly. 'I wonder now if it wasn't what he wanted, if he didn't confide certain things to me knowingly, to drive me to it.'

'Did you call your sister to give yourself an alibi?'

She nodded again.

'I assume you went downstairs when you left the boudoir on the pretext of making toddies?' Maigret went on.

He saw her frown, and her gaze turned away from Gouin and came to rest on Maigret. She seemed to hesitate. You sensed there was a struggle in her. At last, in a curt voice, she said:

'It isn't true.'

'What isn't true?'

'That my sister stayed on her own.'

As Gouin looked at him with an ironic glint in his eyes, Maigret turned red, because that look clearly meant:

'What did I tell you?'

It was true, Germaine was refusing to bear the weight of the crime alone. She could have just kept silent, but she had to speak out.

'Antoinette knew what I was going to do. My courage failed me at the last moment, so she went down with me.'

'Did she go in?'

'She stayed on the stairs.'

And after a silence, as if defying all of them:

'Too bad! It's the truth.'

Her lips were trembling with contained rage.

'Now he'll be able to renew his harem!'

Madame Gouin was wrong. There was little change in the professor's life. It was not until a few months later that Lucile Decaux moved in with him, while continuing to be his assistant and secretary.

Did she try to get him to marry her? Maigret had no idea.

In any case, the professor did not remarry.

And whenever his name came up in conversation, Maigret pretended not to hear, or hastened to talk about something else.